"I swore I would one day make you pay for what you did to me, Ava, and that day has come," he said. "This villa is mine and so is everything in it—including you."

She swallowed convulsively as she tried to pull out of his hold. "No…no!"

"Yes and yes, *ma belle*," he said. "Do you not want to hear my terms?"

Ava fought for control of her emotions. "Go on, then," she said, dropping her shoulders slightly.

His fingers relaxed their hold, his thumb moving in a slow caress over the pillow of her bottom lip until every nerve was tingling. Ava was mesmerized by his touch. It was so achingly gentle after his flaying words. She felt herself melting, the stiffness going out of her limbs, her body remembering how it felt to press up against his hard, protective warmth.

After a moment he seemed to check himself. His hand dropped from her mouth and his eyes hardened to black coal again. "You will be my mistress," he said. "I will pay you an allowance for as long as we are together. But I would like to make one thing very clear from the outset. Unlike the way you manipulated Cole into marrying you, I will not be offering the same deal. There will be no marriage between us. Ever."

All about the author...
Melanie Milburne

MELANIE MILBURNE read her first Harlequin® novel when she was seventeen and has never looked back. She decided she would settle for nothing less than a tall, dark and handsome hero as her future husband. Well, she's not only still reading romance but writing it, as well! And the tall, dark and handsome hero? She fell in love with him on the second date and was secretly engaged to him within six weeks.

Two sons later, they arrived in Hobart, Tasmania— the jewel in the Australian crown. Once their boys were safely in school, Melanie went back to university and received her bachelor's and master's degrees.

As part of her final assessment she conducted a tutorial on the romance genre. As she was reading a paragraph from the novel of a prominent Harlequin® author, the door suddenly burst open. The husband she thought was working was actually standing there dressed in a tuxedo, his dark brown eyes centered on her startled blue ones. He strode purposefully across the room, hauled Melanie into his arms and kissed her deeply and passionately before setting her back down and leaving without a single word. The lecturer gave Melanie a high distinction and her fellow students gave her jealous glares! And so her pilgrimage into romance writing was set!

Melanie also enjoys long-distance running and is a nationally ranked top-ten swimmer in Australia. She learned to swim as an adult, so for anyone out there who thinks they can't do something—you can! Her motto is "Don't say I can't; say I CAN TRY."

Melanie Milburne

CASTELLANO'S MISTRESS OF REVENGE

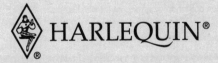

HARLEQUIN®

TORONTO • NEW YORK • LONDON
AMSTERDAM • PARIS • SYDNEY • HAMBURG
STOCKHOLM • ATHENS • TOKYO • MILAN • MADRID
PRAGUE • WARSAW • BUDAPEST • AUCKLAND

Recycling programs
for this product may
not exist in your area.

ISBN-13: 978-0-373-23720-3

CASTELLANO'S MISTRESS OF REVENGE

First North American Publication 2010.

Printed in U.S.A.

CASTELLANO'S MISTRESS
OF REVENGE

To my beautiful friend, Louise Gordon. You are such a giving soul, so gentle and understanding and so non-judgmental. You have supported me through some very dark times and I dedicate this book to you in honor of our friendship.

CHAPTER ONE

'OF COURSE, Madame Cole, you get to keep the jewellery and any other personal gifts Mr Cole gave to you during your marriage,' the lawyer said as he closed the thick document folder in front of him. 'But the Monte Carlo villa and the yacht, as well as Mr Cole's entire business portfolio, now belong to Signor Marcelo Castellano.'

Ava sat very still and composed in her chair. She had trained herself over the years to keep her emotions under strict control. No flicker of fear showed in her eyes, and no tremble of her neatly manicured hands as they lay elegantly on her lap betrayed her. But, deep inside her chest, her heart felt as if a large hand had closed over it and begun to squeeze it with a brutal strength. 'I understand,' she said in a coolly detached tone. 'I am in the process of making arrangements for my things to be moved from the villa as soon as possible.'

'Signor Castellano has insisted you do not leave the villa until he meets with you there,' the lawyer said. 'Apparently there are things he wishes to discuss with you to do with the handover of the property.'

This time it was almost impossible to control the widening of her eyes as she looked across the wide desk at Monsieur Letourneur. 'I am sure the household staff will be perfectly capable of giving him a guided tour,' she said, tying her hands together to stop them from fidgeting with her bag.

'Nevertheless he insisted on seeing you in person, at 8:00 p.m. this evening,' Monsieur Letourneur said. 'I believe he wants to move in immediately.'

Ava stared at the lawyer, her heart starting to flap in panic. 'Is that legal?' she asked. 'The short-term lease on an apartment I had lined up fell through and I haven't had time to search for an alternative. There's been so much to do and I—'

'It is perfectly legal,' Monsieur Letourneur said with a hint of impatience. 'He has owned the villa for several months now, even before your husband passed away. In any case, a letter was sent to you a few weeks ago to inform you of Signor Castellano's intention to take possession.'

Ava felt her insides turn somersaults, not smoothly executed ones, but jerky and uncoordinated tumbles that left her feeling dizzy. She stared at the lawyer, unable to speak, barely able to think. What was she to do? Where was she to go at such short notice? She had money in her account, but certainly not enough to pay for a hotel for days, perhaps even weeks on end whilst searching for a place to live.

Right from the start Douglas had insisted on everything being in his name. That had been part of the deal he had made when insisting she become his wife. Then upon his death there had been so many expenses with the funeral and the outstanding bills he had left unattended to in the last stages of his illness.

'But I received no such letter!' she finally said when she could get her thoughts into some sort of working order. 'Are you sure one was sent?'

The lawyer opened the file in front of him and passed her a copy of a computer-written letter which confirmed her worst nightmare.

Somehow the letter must have gone astray, for she had never received it. She stared at the words printed there, unable to believe this was happening to her.

'I believe you have a history with Signor Castellano, *oui*?' The lawyer's voice jolted her out of her anguished rumination.

'*Oui, monsieur,*' she said with a frown still pulling at her brow. 'Five years ago…' she swallowed tightly '…in London.'

'I am sorry things did not work out better for you, Madame Cole,' the lawyer said. 'Mr Cole's wishes were for you to be well provided for, but the global financial crisis hit him very hard, as indeed it did many investors and business people. It was fortunate Signor Castellano agreed to cover the remaining debts as part of the takeover package.'

Ava's stomach suddenly dropped like a faulty elevator. 'D-debts?' The word came out of her parched mouth like a ghostly whisper. 'But I thought everything had been seen to. Douglas assured me everything was sorted out, that there would be nothing to worry about.' Even as she said the words she realised how stupid and naïve she sounded. She sounded exactly like the empty-headed trophy wife the Press had always made her out to be. But then didn't she deserve the slight? After all, she had been a naïve fool to take Douglas at his word five years ago, only to find out within hours of marrying him his word was not to be trusted.

Monsieur Letourneur looked at her gravely. 'Perhaps he did not wish to distress you with how bad things were towards the end. But let me tell you, without Signor Castellano's generous offer you would be in very deep water indeed. Every financial institution in the world is jumpy these days. Margin calls are happening almost daily. Signor Castellano has agreed to cover all future requests for payment.'

Ava quickly ran the tip of her tongue across what remained of her lip gloss, tasting a sweet and sour cocktail of strawberries and fear. 'That seems rather generous of him,' she said, keeping her shoulders straight and her spine even straighter.

'Yes, but then he is one of the richest men in Europe,' the lawyer said. 'His construction company has grown phenomenally over the last few years. He has branches all over the world, even in your country of birth, I understand. Do you intend to return to Australia now?'

Ava thought longingly of returning to her land of birth, but with her younger sister now married and based in London, she felt it was too far to relocate, especially now. Serena wasn't back on her feet after suffering from a devastating miscarriage after yet another failed IVF attempt. Ava had not long returned from visiting Serena and had promised to come back as soon as she could to help her through such a harrowing time. But going there now was out of the question. Serena would immediately sense something was up and it would not do her recovery any good to find out about the mess Ava was in. 'No,' she said. 'I have a friend I would like to visit in Scotland. I thought I might try and find a job while I am there.'

Ava could see the cynicism in the lawyer's eyes as he got to his feet. She supposed from his perspective she deserved it; after all, she had to all intents and purposes been a kept woman for the last five years. No doubt he thought finding a regular job with the sort of perks she had been used to was not going to be easy.

Ava was well aware of the precarious position she was in. It *wasn't* going to be easy, but she needed a regular flow of income to help her sister have the baby she so desperately wanted. Her husband, Richard Holt, earned a reasonable income as an academic, but nowhere near enough to cover the expense of repeated IVF treatments.

Ava glanced at her watch as she left the lawyer's building. She had less than three hours until she saw Marc Castellano for the first time in five years. Her stomach fluttered with feathered wings of fear as her footsteps click-clacked along the pavement.

Fear, or was it excitement?

It was perhaps a perverse bit of both, Ava acceded. She had more or less been expecting him to contact her. She knew he would relish in the opportunity to gloat over the way things had turned out for her. The news of Douglas's death six weeks ago had gone around the world. Why Marc had waited this long to see her she supposed was all part of his plan to make the most of her very public fall.

The villa was cool after the heat of the summer sun and she released her sticky hair from the back of her collar, rolling her neck and shoulders to try and ease some of the tension that had gathered there.

The housekeeper, an older French woman called Celeste, came towards her from the main reception room at the foot of the grand staircase. *'Excusez-moi, madame, mais vous avez un visiteur,'* she said and, changing to English, continued, 'Signor Marcelo Castellano. He said you were expecting him.'

Ava felt a scuttle-like sensation pass across her scalp, like tiny panicked feet tripping through her hair. *'Merci, Celeste,'* she said, placing her bag on the nearest surface with a hand that was almost but not quite steady, 'but I was led to understand he was coming much later.'

The housekeeper raised her hands in a what-would-I-know? gesture. 'He is here now, in there.' She pointed to the formal reception room that overlooked the gardens and the port and sea beyond.

Ava set her mouth, although her heart gave another flip-flop-like beat. 'You can leave now,' she said. 'I will see you in the morning. *Bonsoir.'*

The housekeeper gave a respectful nod of her salt-and-pepper head and backed away. Ava drew in a breath, held it for a beat or two before releasing it in a jagged stream.

The door of the reception room was closed, but she could sense Marc standing the other side of it. He wouldn't be sitting. He wouldn't be pacing impatiently either. He would be standing.

Waiting.

For her.

Putting one high-heeled foot in front of the other, Ava moved to the door and, opening it, walked into the room.

The first thing she noticed was his smell: citrus and sharp with an undertone of masculine body heat, it played about her nostrils, teasing them into an involuntary flare.

The next thing she noticed was his eyes. They locked on hers within a heartbeat, deep and dark as blackened coal, inscrutable and yet dangerously sexy. Fringed with thick black lashes beneath equally dark brows, his gaze was both intelligent and astute and intensely, unmistakably male. After holding hers for what seemed an eternity, his gaze then went on to sweep over her lazily, leaving a trail of blistering heat in its wake. Flames erupted beneath her skin, licking along her veins, lighting a fire of need deep and low inside her that she had thought had long ago turned to ashes.

He was wearing a dark charcoal-grey finely pinstriped suit, which showcased the breadth of his shoulders and the taut leanness of his frame. His ink-black hair was longer than he had worn it in the past, but Ava thought the slightly tousled just-out-of-bed look suited him perfectly. His crisply white shirt and silver-embossed tie emphasised his olive skin, the shiny cufflinks at his strongly boned wrists a touch of class that reminded her of how incredibly successful he had become over the last five years.

'So, we finally meet again,' Marc said in that deep, husky male tone that had always made her spine feel watery and unstable. 'I am sorry I didn't make it to the funeral or send you a card with my condolences.' He gave a small movement of his lips which belied the sincerity of his statement. 'Under the circumstances I didn't think either would be appropriate.'

Ava pulled her shoulders back to counter-act his effect on her. 'I suppose you are only here now to gloat over your prize,' she said with an attempt at haughtiness.

His dark eyes glittered meaningfully. 'That depends on which prize you are refer-ring to, *ma petite.*'

Ava felt her skin burn as his eyes ran over

her again. It had always made her heart skip when he used French endearments in that sexy Italian accent of his.

She wondered if he knew how much it hurt to see him again. Not just emotionally, but physically. It was like an ache deep in her bones; they creaked with the memory of him holding her, kissing her, making her body explode with passion time and time again. She felt the sharp twinge of response even now by being in the same room as him. It was like strings being tugged deep inside of her, reminding her of all the heat and fire of his desire for her, and hers for him.

She had hoped he would have stopped hating her by now, but she could see the fire of it in his eyes, she could even feel it in the stance of his six-foot-four frame, the tension in his sculptured muscles, and the clenching and unclenching of his long-fingered hands as if he didn't trust himself not to reach out and shake her for how she had betrayed him. If only he knew the truth, but how could she explain it now, after all this time?

Ava raised her chin with a bravado she was nowhere near feeling. 'Let's not speak in riddles, Marc. Say what you came here to say.'

He stepped closer. It was only one step, but

it halted the breath in her throat. She swallowed, but it only made the restriction tighter. She had to crane her neck, for even in her heels he towered over her. His eyes bored into hers, dark and deep pools of simmering anger.

'I am here to take possession of this villa,' he said, 'and to offer you a job for which we both know you are highly qualified.'

She frowned at him, her stomach curdling with unease, her skin tightening all over with apprehension. 'D-doing what?'

His top lip lifted, his eyes glittering with icy disdain. 'Servicing a rich man's needs. You are well known for it, are you not?'

Ava felt a tremor in her spine as his hatred smashed over her in soundless waves. 'You know nothing of my relationship with Douglas,' she said, trying to keep her voice steady and controlled.

'Your meal ticket is dead,' Marc said bluntly. 'He's left you with nothing, not even a roof over your beautiful blonde head.'

'Only because you took it all off him,' she shot back. 'You did it deliberately, didn't you? There were hundreds if not thousands of companies going for the asking, but you hunted him down and took everything off him to get at me.'

He smiled a victor's smile, but there was a hint of cruelty about it. 'I will give you a minute or two to think it over,' he said. 'I am sure you will come to see it as the most sensible course of action at this point in your life.'

'I don't need even a second to think it over,' Ava said through tight lips. 'I don't want your rubbish job.'

A lightning flash of fury lit his gaze from behind. 'Did your lawyer not explain to you how things are?'

'I would rather live on the streets than work in any capacity for you,' she said. 'I know what you're trying to do, Marc, but it won't work. I know you think I deliberately betrayed you, but that's not the way it was. I knew nothing of Douglas's business interests. He didn't tell me he was bidding for the same contract as you.'

His mouth was a thin, flat line of tension. 'You double-crossing liar,' he ground out venomously. 'You did everything in your power to ruin me and you damned near got away with it. I lost nearly everything. *Everything*, do you hear me?'

Ava closed her eyes in distress. The vibration of his anger in the air was like pummelling blows to her flesh. She could not defend herself against her guilt at what she had inadvertently done to him by marrying Douglas Cole. But given her time again she would still have done it, for Serena's sake.

'Open your eyes,' Marc growled at her.

Her eyes sprang open, the nettle-like sting of tears blurring her vision. 'Don't do this, Marc,' she said, close to pleading. 'The past can't be changed by manipulating things now.'

His eyes blazed like twin black bowls of flame as he grasped her chin between two of his fingers, his touch like a blistering brand on her skin. His eyes drilled into hers, holding hers in a duel she could never hope to win. She lowered her lashes, but he countered it by pushing her chin even higher. 'I swore I would one day make you pay for what you did to me, Ava, and that day has come,' he said. 'This villa is mine and everything in it, including you.'

She swallowed convulsively as she tried to pull out of his hold. 'No…*no*!'

His fingers bit into her flesh. 'Yes and yes, *ma belle*,' he said. 'Do you not want to hear my terms?'

Ava fought for control of her emotions. She bit the inside of her lip, tasting blood and the bitterness of regret. 'Go on, then,' she said, dropping her shoulders slightly.

His fingers relaxed their hold, his thumb moving in a slow caress over the pillow of her bottom lip until every nerve-end was tingling. Ava was mesmerised by his touch. It was so achingly gentle after his flaying words. She felt herself melting, the stiffness going out of her limbs, her body remembering how it felt to press up against his hard, protective warmth.

After a moment he seemed to check himself. His hand dropped from her mouth and his eyes hardened to black coal again. 'You will be my mistress,' he said. 'I will pay you an allowance for as long as we are together. But I would like to make one thing very clear from the outset. Unlike the way you manipulated Cole into marrying you, I will not be offering the same deal. There will be no marriage between us. Ever.'

Ava felt her heart contract in pain at the bitterness in his tone. He had spoken the words like a business plan. But then, what had changed? Hadn't he said much the same five years ago? No marriage, no kids, no commitment. And she had been foolish enough to accept it…for a time.

Ava drew in a breath that scalded her

throat. 'You seem very convinced I will accept your offer.'

'That is because I know you, Ava,' he said with a sardonic light in his gaze. 'You need money and a lot of it.'

'I can find work.' Pride pulled her shoulders back even farther. 'I've been thinking of returning to modelling.'

A determined look hardened his eyes to black ice. 'One word from me and there's not an agency the length and breadth of Europe who would take you on.'

Ava wished she had the courage to call his bluff. But after a five-year hiatus in her modelling career at Douglas's insistence she didn't like her chances of being picked up by her old agency, let alone anyone else.

'I can find other work,' she said with a defiant look.

'Not the sort of work that will pay you enough to regularly top up your sister's bank account.'

Ava felt her eyes widen. 'You *know* about that?'

He gave her an enigmatic look. 'You know the saying—keep your friends close but your enemies closer. I am making it my business to find out everything there is to find out about you, Ava.'

Ava felt as if he had pierced her heart with a long metal skewer. She felt the barb of it right to her backbone; it reverberated throughout her body, making her want to hug her arms around herself, to stop the pulse of pain. But somehow she stood firm, her eyes holding the black fire of his.

'Please keep Serena out of this,' she said hollowly.

'There will be no need for her to know anything other than we are together again,' he said.

Ava wondered how the news would affect her sister. Serena had out of fierce loyalty never mentioned Marc's name in her presence over the last five years. She had also kept the secret of Ava's real relationship with Douglas Cole quiet, so quiet her husband, Richard, was to this day unaware of it. Serena had been too terrified Richard's conservative family would be totally scandalised by her near-brush with a prison term that only Ava's actions had rescued her from experiencing.

But returning to Marc on the terms he had outlined was unthinkable to Ava. How would she bear his daily quest for revenge? How could she face that hatred day after day?

She looked up at him again, shocked at how cold and ruthlessly calculating he had become. He had certainly been no angel in the past—yes, he had been strong-willed and proud and had arrogantly insisted on his own way, but he had never been cruel. But what hurt most was that it was her choice to marry Douglas that had brought about the change in him. Of course Marc would think it had been deliberate, but then, unbeknown to her, Douglas had planned it that way.

She twisted her hands, unconsciously fingering the amethyst ring on her finger, a peace offering Douglas had given her during the last months of his illness. 'I need some time to think about this…'

Marc's eyes flashed like fast-drawn daggers. 'You've had six weeks.'

Ava blinked at the savage bite of his words. 'You surely don't expect me to accept this outrageous offer without some careful consideration, do you?'

His mouth was curled upwards in a sneer. 'It didn't take you too long to consider moving on with another man after you walked out on me. Within a month you were living with Cole as his wife.'

'I am sure you moved on with your life just as quickly,' she said with a fiery flash of her eyes. 'In fact you are rarely out of the Press with a starlet on your arm.'

'I admit I do not live the life of a monk,' he said, 'which brings me to another condition of mine on the arrangement.'

'I haven't agreed to it yet.'

'You will.'

Ava ground her teeth at his imperious manner. 'Let me guess,' she said, glaring at him resentfully. 'You want me to be faithful to you while you get to do whatever you like with whomever you like.'

His dark eyes gleamed. 'You are well trained, I see. Perhaps your time with Cole has finally taught you how to behave.'

She tightened her lips until they went numb, anger bubbling inside her at his assumption of her as a gold-digger. It was so unfair. Why couldn't he leave the past alone? To come to her now, after all this time, was going to achieve nothing but more heartache for her. It had broken her heart to walk away from him the first time. It had taken every bit of willpower and self-respect to do so.

Living as his mistress had been so bitter-sweet and in the end she had chosen the bitter over the sweet. He had flatly refused to promise her anything but a short-term affair. The concept of marriage was anathema to him; now it seemed more so than ever.

Marc took an envelope out of his jacket pocket and handed it to her. 'I have drawn up a legal document for you to sign,' he said. 'It states how much money I am willing to pay you to cohabit with me. By signing it you will be unable to claim support when our relationship is terminated.'

'A prenuptial?' she asked, frowning as her fingers took the envelope from him.

'Without the nuptials,' he said, his eyes diamond-hard. 'No marriage, no children.'

Ava felt her insides twist in pain. Watching her sister go through the agony of not being able to conceive had made her acutely aware of how much she longed to have a baby of her own. To hear Marc state so implacably that he wanted no children struck at the heart of her. She was twenty-seven years old, which was still young enough not to panic, but with her *younger* sister's fertility problems she couldn't quite quell the worry that she too might not be able to conceive naturally.

'I can assure you I would not for a moment think of bringing a child into such an arrangement as this,' she said, turning away from Marc to put the envelope to one side.

Ava heard him move behind her and froze. She silently prayed for him not to touch her in case she betrayed herself. The skin along her bare arms crawled with anticipation of his warm, gliding hands. How many times had he embraced her from behind in the past? His hands would move slowly from her hips to her breasts, cupping her, his mouth nuzzling on the sensitive skin of her neck until she would turn in his arms and offer herself to him.

Her mind exploded with images of them together. The passion he had ignited in her was something she had never experienced before even though she had not been a virgin when they had met.

When his hands came to rest on her hips she shuddered. 'You find my touch abhorrent, or is it that you are still hungry for it?' he asked, his warm hint-of-mint breath skating past her ear.

If only he knew! she thought as her heart

rammed against her sternum like a giant pendulum inside the body of a too small clock. 'I told you…I…I want some time to think about this,' she said, trying to keep her voice even.

He turned her around to face him, his eyes boring into hers. 'You haven't got time to think about it, *cara*,' he said. 'You have debts up to your diamond-studded ears.' He fingered one glittering earlobe. 'Did he buy these for you?'

Ava's breath caught in her throat like a scrap of silk on a savage thorn. 'Y-yes…'

His hands fell to his sides as he commanded, 'Take them off.'

She frowned again, her stomach nosediving in alarm. 'What?'

His mouth was bracketed by lines of steel. 'Take them off and everything else he gave you. *Now*.'

Ava pressed her lips together to contain her pulsing panic. Was this really her Marc? The man she had fallen in love with so deeply and irrevocably? He was a stranger to her now, a terrifying stranger with not just revenge on his mind, but the total humiliation of her as well.

She would not give in to him.

She would not.

She tightened her hands into fists by her sides, holding his glacial glare with a feisty flash of her own. 'No.' Her voice came out too thready and soft, so she repeated it. 'No. Absolutely not.'

His pupils flared, his mouth flattening even further. 'I will give you one minute, Ava, otherwise the deal is off. Keep in mind the massive debts your husband left behind. At last count it was in the hundreds of thousands.' He set the timer on his watch, his dark gaze holding hers challengingly. 'Your minute starts now.'

She swallowed back her anguish, the determination in his eyes making the base of her spine rattle in fear. 'D-don't do this, Marc….'

A nerve flickered at the side of his mouth. 'If you will not do it then I will do it for you,' he warned.

Ava believed him well capable of it. Her hands began to tremble as she tried to remove the earrings, her fingers fumbling uselessly until she felt terrifyingly close to tears. She soldiered on, glaring at him bitterly, hating him with such intensity she could taste the acridity of it in her mouth.

Finally she got the studs out and placed them on the coffee table to her right.

'Now the rest,' he said, standing with his feet apart, his arms folded across his chest in an authoritarian stance that boiled her blood.

Still glaring at him, she took each of her dress rings off and put them beside the earrings. 'There,' she said, arching one of her brows at him. 'Happy now?'

His black eyes stripped her mercilessly. 'Keep going.'

Ava's heart lurched against her chest wall. She sent the point of her tongue out over her lips, buying for time, wondering if he wanted her to crumble emotionally, to beg and to plead with him to stop.

She would *not* do it.

She would *not* bend or break, she would *not* cry, she would *not* beg.

She raised her chin and locked gazes with him. Blue-grey warred with black-brown for a pulsing moment. 'All right, then,' she said with a devil-may-care lift of one shoulder as she loosened the catch on her watch. She slipped it off her wrist and placed it beside the earrings and rings.

She straightened and, giving him a challenging look, slipped off her shoes, kicking them to one side before she reached for the zipper at the back of her skirt. She told herself she had stood undressed in front of hundreds of people before while she had been modelling. This would be no different; besides, he had seen it all before. Her body was no secret to him. He knew every curve and contour and every secret place.

The tension in the air was palpable.

Ava slid the zipper down, the metallic sound thunderous in the crackling silence. The fabric slipped to the floor and she stepped out of its circle, her fingers going to the hem of her pull-on top.

Marc's eyes followed her like a night-vision searchlight. She felt the heat of it scorch her flesh as her top joined her skirt on the floor. She stood before him in a black, French, lace push-up bra and knickers, her chin high, her right hip tilted in a model-like pose. 'I bought these myself,' she said with a defiant look.

His lips flickered, his dark eyes gleaming. 'Prove it.'

Ava clenched her teeth, fighting to keep her cool. He wanted her to fall apart, she had to remember that. He wanted her pride any way he could get it. 'I don't have the receipt any more, so I am afraid you will have to take my word for it,' she said, pushing up her chin to disguise its wobble.

'Your word?' His top lip lifted in a mocking curl. 'Since when should I take as gospel the word of a gold-digger?'

'I am not a gold-digger,' she said with quiet but steely dignity.

The timer on his watch beeped, informing her the minute was up.

Ava felt her stomach slip as Marc's gaze hit hers. 'Well?' he said.

She had never felt so naked and exposed in her life and yet she was still wearing more than most people wore on the French Riviera beaches she could see from the villa windows.

'How much are you going to pay me?' she asked, knowing it would be exactly the question a gold-digger would ask, but she was beyond caring. Serena was more important than her pride at this point. What her sister had suffered recently was far worse than anything Marc Castellano could do to her.

He named a sum that lifted her brows. 'Th-that much?' she asked in a croak.

He gave her an imperious smile, the black holes of his pupils flaring with passionate promise. 'I am going to make you earn every penny of it, Ava. I don't suppose you have forgotten how good we were together, hmm?'

Ava felt her cheeks flame with colour. She remembered everything: every touch, every kiss, every incendiary caress and every earth-shattering orgasm that had left her quaking in his arms time and time again. 'You want some sort of medal for being able to perform an act that humans, even the most base of animals, have been doing for centuries?' she asked with a cutting look.

He suddenly snagged one of her wrists and pulled her up against him, his chest to her pounding chest and his strong, im-movable thighs to her weak, trembling ones. 'Don't push me too far, Ava,' he said in a low growl. 'I am this close,' he held up his index finger and thumb a pinch distance apart, 'to walking out of here and leaving you to face your sugar daddy's creditors.'

Again Ava desperately wanted to call his bluff. She would have if it hadn't been for Serena. A vision of her shattered sister, holding the ultrasound picture of the baby she had lost, was the only thing that stopped her. 'All right,' she said on an expelled breath. 'I'll do it.'

Marc's hold loosened, but he didn't release her. Instead his thumb found her thundering pulse, stroking over it in a rhythmic motion that was as powerful as a drug. 'I will release a Press statement for tomorrow's papers,' he said into the silence. 'We will begin living together as of now.'

Ava looked up at him in wide-eyed trepidation. 'So…so soon?'

His eyes went to her mouth before returning to hers. 'I have waited five years to have you where I want you,' he said.

She gave him an embittered look. 'Where might that be?' she asked. 'In the palm of your hand, begging for mercy?'

He traced a long finger over each of the upper curves of her breasts before dipping into the valley of her cleavage, the nerves beneath her skin going off like miniature explosives. 'I think you know exactly where I want you,' he said in a tone that was rough and deep and sensually, sinfully dangerous.

Ava felt her body quiver at the thought of him plunging into her, claiming her as his.

Not in love.

Not in mutual attraction.

But in lustful, hate-filled revenge….

CHAPTER TWO

IN SPITE of the warmth of the room Ava felt her skin rise in goose pimples. She rubbed at her upper arms, trying so hard to hold her ground. Her head was aching with tension, her mind trying to stay clear and focused while the earth seemed to be shifting beneath her feet. The air was fizzing with Marc's hatred, high-voltage waves of it zapping at her, making her skin pepper all the more.

'Are you cold?' Marc asked.

She kept her mouth rigid with anger. 'What is that to you?'

He held her glare for a pulsing moment. 'Have you had dinner?' he asked.

'No, and if you think I am going to dine with you dressed like this you can think again,' she said with a lift of her chin.

He smiled as his gaze raked over her again. 'Delightful as that sounds, no—I will not take you out in public like that. As of this evening your body is for my eyes and my eyes only.'

Ava found it hard to stand still for the rage that was rumbling through her like seismic activity preceding a massive earthquake. 'You know there are probably street workers who come much cheaper than me,' she said, goaded beyond caution.

'Yes, but I want you,' he said with a devilish gleam in his black-as-night gaze. 'We have unfinished business, do we not?'

Ava glared at him. 'Any business we had ended five years ago. I thought I had made that perfectly clear.'

His top lip lifted in disgust. 'Oh, yes, by moving out of the apartment I had set up for you without even telling me to my face. I came home to find the place empty apart from a note.'

Ava felt a twinge of guilt about not meeting him face-to-face back then, but she knew if she had he would have persuaded her to stay with him. A note had seemed safer, she'd had more control, the sort of control she had lost the moment she had met and fallen in love with him. She had been so weak where he was concerned, and, although she had put it down to her youth at the time, seeing him again frightened her that it might very well happen all over again. She had come full circle. The irony of it was beyond painful; it was like a razor blade stuck sideways in her throat. She felt as if she could taste the blood of its embedment, the bitter, metallic taste of regret and heartbreak at what she had lost by leaving him, and yet here she was, back in his life and under his command.

Ava lowered her gaze from the accusing glare of Marc's. 'I'm sorry,' she said, but it came out grudgingly and not at all convincing.

Marc watched as she stood before him with her bottom lip trembling, her heart-shaped face pale, and her grey-blue eyes like lakes of shimmering liquid.

He turned away, his anger making his movements stiff and jerky. He clenched and unclenched his hands, wanting to punch deep holes in the walls in frustration and fury. It sickened him that he had allowed her to drop his guard. For years he had sworn he would not do as his father had done: become totally captivated by a woman who couldn't be trusted.

His mother had slept her way through his childhood with an array of other men until she finally left the family home when Marc was seven years old. He could still recall the last time he saw her at the age of ten, getting into the top-of-the-range sports car of her latest rich toy-boy lover, waving at Marc as they drove off to their deaths three hours later on the Amalfi Coast. He had spent the next decade of his life trying to prop up the shattered shell of his father until death—with the aid of large amounts of alcohol—had finally claimed him.

Marc had waited for five years to avenge his bludgeoned pride against Ava McGuire. Five years of meticulously planning his revenge. Step by step he had rebuilt his empire, taking the greatest pleasure in finally bringing Douglas Cole to his knees, with a little help from the stock-market volatility.

Of all the people for her to marry, Ava could not have chosen a better way of ensuring Marc hated her for life. He loathed thinking about his arch enemy making love to her. His mind revolted at the thought of that bloated body heaving over her slim form. But then she was a gold-digger who would always sell herself to the highest bidder. She had just proved it by the way she had agreed to his terms. She had openly taunted him with her beautiful body, but he was not going to take what was on offer until he was good and ready. He wanted her, it was like a virulent fever in his blood, but he was not going to give in to it until she begged him to make love to her. But this time around it would not be making love; it would be sex, nothing but pure physical need that he would enjoy until he tired of her. She would not be the one to walk out on him the way his harlot of a mother had done to his father. This time around Marc would call an end to the relationship when he was satisfied he was over her.

He turned from the view at the windows and faced her. 'I want this placed stripped of everything that belonged to Cole,' he said. 'I have a removals van waiting outside to take everything away in order for my things to be brought in.'

Her slim throat rose and fell over a swallow. 'There's not much left of Douglas's things,' she said. 'Since the funeral I have sorted through it all and sent it to his ex-wife and children. The furniture came with the villa when he purchased it.'

'You have met his ex-wife and family?' Marc asked, his brows lifting in mild surprise.

She swept the point of her tongue across her lips, swallowing again. 'Yes, at the funeral. They came all the way from Perth in Australia. Mrs…' She hesitated for a fraction of a second before continuing, 'Renata Cole was very pleasant. Adam and Lucy, his adult children, too, were very gracious.'

'Considering their father had shacked up with a tart,' he said, watching as her cheeks bloomed with colour.

'Is this to be part of the deal between us?' she asked with a defiant spark in her grey-blue eyes. 'For you to insult me at every available opportunity?'

He ignored her comment to say, 'You will no longer be using Cole's name. It is in the legal document I gave you. You are to revert to your maiden name even though you are anything but a maiden.'

She opened her mouth to protest, but he cut her off curtly. 'Go and get dressed. I have made a booking at a restaurant for dinner.'

Her eyes rounded. 'You were *that* sure I would agree to this preposterous plan?'

'But of course, *ma belle*,' he said with a mocking smile. He patted where his wallet was inside his suit jacket pocket. 'After all, money is the thing you most desire, is it not?'

Her eyes were like twin tornadoes, darkening with fury. 'Doesn't it make a difference to know I don't want it for myself?' she bit out through tight lips.

He gave a couldn't-care-less shrug. 'It is of no importance to me what or who you want it for. I understand the thickness of family blood even though I do not have a sibling. As it stands, I am happy to pay you to entertain me, but only until such time as I feel it is time to call it quits.'

The look she gave him would have sliced through steel. 'You mean when you've ground my pride into the dust.'

Marc moved his lips from side to side, reining in his temper. She had some nerve to lament the damage to her pride, considering what she had done to his. 'I have already told you to go and get dressed,' he said. 'I would advise you to do so and now, otherwise I may very well change my mind and take you dressed as you are.'

She turned with a swish of her shoulder-length blonde hair and padded up the sweeping staircase, the action of her endless legs and neat bottom making the blood surge to his groin.

He shoved his hands deep in his trouser

pockets to stop himself from reaching for her as he so often had done in the past. He'd had lovers since, but no one made his blood heat the way Ava McGuire's did. All she had to do was look at him from those smoky grey-blue eyes of hers and he was rock-hard. He sucked in a harsh breath, fighting against the flood of memories, but it was impossible to mentally sandbag against such powerful sensual recollections. For five years they had tortured him, making him ache with the need to feel her again, to have her in his arms, to hold her and have his fill of her.

He ran a hand through the thickness of his hair as he paced the floor again. He would get her out of his system this time once and for all. Whatever it took, he would do it.

He *had* to in order to move on with his life. This was his last chance and he was going to make the most of every single minute.

Ava dressed in a slim-fitting black cocktail dress from her short-lived modelling days and, slipping her feet into heels, picked up a small evening bag.

She glanced at her reflection in the mirror, grimacing at the state of her hair. She put her bag down and quickly ran a brush through her tresses so they fell about her shoulders in casual waves. Apart from a dusting of mineral make-up and a quick dab of lip gloss she left the rest of her face alone. It wouldn't matter what she did to herself—she was never going to be good enough for Marc Castellano, she thought with aching sadness. He enjoyed the company of beautiful women all over the world, women who willingly grasped at the chance to hang off his arm or slip between the sheets of his bed. Ava's stomach hollowed in anguish at the thought of how many had been there since she had been his mistress. The thought of him touching others the way he had touched her made her feel as if her heart was being wrenched in two. She had tried over the years not to think of it; every time she saw a Press photo of him with yet another glamorous woman on his arm she had quickly turned the page, suppressing the wave of longing until it finally subsided.

When she came down the stairs, Marc was speaking to a man who was dressed in a removals company uniform, the first of some items already placed in the foyer in cardboard boxes.

Ava's stomach clenched at the thought of how quickly things had changed. Marc had wasted no time in taking possession of the villa; how soon would he insist on the other more intimate terms of the deal? In the past she had shared his bed with love, or at least on her part. But how could she possibly share it with the hatred that bubbled like volcanic mud between them now?

Marc dismissed the man and turned as she came down the last of the stairs, his dark gaze running over her in hot-blooded appraisal. 'Very nice,' he said. 'But then you have always had the amazing ability to look glamorous in whatever you are wearing—' his eyes glinted as he added '—or not wearing.'

Ava hoisted her chin at a haughty height. 'In case you are wondering, this dress is mine.'

'Yes, I know,' he said. 'I recognise it from our first meeting.'

She tried to hide her reaction to his statement, but it was almost impossible to control the flip and flop and flutter of her pulse. That he remembered such a minor detail made her wonder if he had cared more for her back then than he had let on at the time. He had always seemed so aloof and non-committal when it came to his feelings. She on the other hand had been effusive with stating hers, which had made her feel gauche and immature. She wished she had been a little more sophisticated back then. If only she had been able to look upon their affair as a casual fling she might not have had her hopes crushed so badly. But from the moment their eyes had met across a crowded bar she had felt something fall into place deep inside her. No one else had had that effect on her and after all this time she had come to the conclusion no one else ever would.

Ava followed him out of the villa to a waiting car outside. The driver held the door open for her and waited while she took her seat, with Marc joining her, his long, strong thighs brushing against hers.

He took one of her hands in his, holding her lightly, but with an undercurrent of strength that silently warned her not to try and pull away.

Ava thought of all the times they had dined together in the past. The romantic candlelit dinners where she had gazed into his eyes, his fingers lazily stroking hers, making her heart thud in anticipation of returning to the apartment to make love into the early hours of the morning.

She wondered if he was thinking of those times now. It was so hard to tell what was going on behind the hard mask of his face. He was just as heart-stoppingly gorgeous as before. The faint shadow of regrowth on his jaw made her fingers itch to touch him, to feel that sexy stubble under the soft pads of her fingertips. Her body trembled at the memory of how it had felt to feel his unshaven skin against her inner thighs as he pleasured her with his lips and tongue.

She crossed her legs, trying to quell the pulse of her body, but with him sitting so close it was like trying to stop ice melting under the flare of a blowtorch.

Marc lifted her hand to his mouth, the point of his tongue dipping between the sensitive web between her index and thumb. It was the merest touch, a hot, moist hint of what was to come. Ava shivered and closed her eyes tightly, calling upon every bit of willpower she possessed not to turn in her seat and place her mouth greedily against his.

He kept her hand in his, idly toying with her fingers, outlining the smoothly manicured shape of her nails. Ava was intensely aware of her forearm resting on his muscular thigh, her hand so close to the hot, hard heat of him she ached to explore him, to see if he was responding to her as she was to him. Her eyes glanced sideways, her heart nearly stopping when she saw the tenting of his trousers. She gulped and quickly looked out of the opposite window, but she heard his low deep chuckle, and felt his fingers tighten as they brought hers to his growing erection.

Her heart thumped as she felt his turgid length, her inner muscles contracting and the dew of desire anointing her in spite of every effort to curb her response to him.

'I can see—or rather, I can feel you haven't lost your touch, *cara*,' he said, keeping her hand against him. 'Tell me, did you ever service Cole in the back of his limousine?'

His crude question was like a slap across the face with an icy hand. She wrenched her hand out of his, wincing as her wrist caught on the metal band of his watch. She glared at him from her corner of the car, holding her wrist with her other hand, her emotions in turmoil as she struggled to keep control.

'Did you?' he asked, his expression hard with bitterness.

'Would you believe me if I said no?' she asked with a challenging look.

His eyes bored into hers as if he was deciding whether to believe her or not. 'You lived with him as his legal wife for five years,' he said. 'I can't imagine there would be much you didn't do with him, especially with the amount of money he spent on you. That's probably why he ended up close to bankruptcy, trying to keep your gold-digging hands full of designer goods.'

'I couldn't give a damn what you think,' she said, searching in her evening bag for a tissue. 'It's pointless discussing anything with you. You've made up your mind and you are never wrong, or so you like to believe.'

Marc frowned as he saw the scratch on the creamy skin of her blue-veined wrist. He took out his handkerchief from his inside pocket and, taking her arm, gently dabbed it. 'It was not my intention to hurt you,' he said.

Her grey-blue eyes glittered. 'That's the whole point of this, isn't it? To hurt me until I finally break.'

He frowned and released her arm, stuffing the used handkerchief in his trouser pocket. 'Perhaps there is a part of me that wants you to suffer the way I suffered,' he said, looking her in the eye. 'But I am not a violent man and you can be assured you will always be absolutely safe with me, Ava.'

Safe? Ava wondered if she could ever be safe from his effect on her. She had told herself over the years she no longer loved him. Denying what she felt for him had been a coping mechanism, a way of navigating herself through the heartbreak of having to leave him while she still could. But in the end it had blown up in her face, for men like Marc Castellano didn't forgive—they got revenge.

She chanced a glance at his brooding expression. He was looking straight ahead, his dark eyes narrowed in fierce concentration, his sensual mouth pulled into an almost straight line. A nerve ticked at the corner of his mouth, like a miniature fist punching beneath the skin.

As if he sensed her eyes on him, he turned and locked gazes. 'Tell me something,' he said, his eyes like steel as they pinned hers. 'Were you involved with Cole the whole time you were seeing me?'

'Of course not.' She bit down on her lip. 'How can you think I would—'

'A month,' he bit out the words as if they were bullets, his black eyes flashing with fury. 'Within a month you were married to that silver-tailed, silver-tongued creep.'

Ava closed her eyes, her head dropping into her hands. 'I can't do this…' Her voice was muffled as she struggled to hold back tears. 'Please take me back to the villa…'

'We are going out to dinner as planned,' he stated intractably.

She lifted her head and threw him a castigating glare. 'You never used to be such an unfeeling bastard, Marc.'

His eyes brewed with resentment. 'It's a bit late to be lamenting my lack of feeling. After all, you were the one who showed me how foolish it is to trust a woman who spouts words of love all the time. But that was your intention from the start, wasn't it? You lured me in and then once you had me dangling on the line you cast me off for a bigger, richer catch.'

Her brow creased in bewilderment. 'Is that what you really think?'

'I should have seen it coming,' he said, throwing his arm along the back of the seat. 'I've had enough gold-diggers try it on me in the past. You were good, I'll grant you that. Convincing and beguiling, and that little lie about only having one lover and it being an unpleasant experience was a nice touch. You really had me going there.'

Ava felt as if he had struck her. The pain she felt at his words was indescribable. He was one of the few people she had told of the night she lost her virginity at the age of nineteen. Even Serena, her sister, didn't know the full details, for Serena had suffered much worse at a much younger age, leaving her scarred and vulnerable for years until she had met Richard. For Marc to throw that confidence back in Ava's face as if it were a fiction to garner sympathy was beyond cruel.

She was glad the driver pulled up in front of the restaurant Marc had chosen, for she was beyond a reply. She got out of the car with stiff movements, not even flinching when Marc took her arm and looped it through his.

The restaurant was crowded, but the table the *maître d'* led them to was in a more secluded area. The lighting was low and intimate, the décor luxurious, the service attentive but not intrusive.

'Would you like an aperitif?' Marc asked after the waiter left them with a drinks menu.

'Soda with a twist of lime,' Ava answered, ignoring the extensive list of alcoholic drinks in front of her.

Marc raised his brows. 'Frightened you might lose your inhibitions and have your wicked way with me?'

She flicked her hair back behind her shoulders, sending him another caustic look. 'You can't make me sleep with you, Marc,' she said.

He leant back in his chair, his gaze running over her tauntingly. 'I don't think it would be too hard to get you begging for it. After all, your sugar daddy has been dead for some weeks now and there has been nothing in the Press about you having found a replacement. A woman like you is not made for celibacy.'

Ava buried her head in the menu rather than meet his sardonic gaze. It annoyed her to think how vulnerable she was to him. Her hand was still tingling from his touch earlier, and her body still smouldering. Every time she chanced a glance at him he seemed to be looking at her mouth, making her lips buzz and swell with anticipation of the passionate pressure of his. She wondered if he was stealthily planning his seduction, taking his time about it to make her feel on tenterhooks. If he was he was certainly succeeding. She could barely sit still in her chair at the thought of him possessing her again. Her inner muscles flickered with an on-off pulse that made it hard for her to concentrate. All she could think of was how it would feel to have him drive into her moist warmth the way he used to do. He was an adventurous lover and yet he could be surprisingly tender too. She had loved that about him, the way he made sure her needs were met before he sought his own release.

What would making love with him now be like? she wondered. Would his quest for revenge make him selfish and demanding instead of considerate and sensually satisfying? Would he treat her like the money-hungry woman he thought she was?

Ava put down the menu with a trembling hand. How had her dreams for a happy life turned into such a nightmare? All she had ever wanted was to find a man who would love her and protect her, to build a family, the sort of family she and Serena had missed out on by the early death of their mother and the rapid remarriage of their father to the woman who had been callously and rather too obviously waiting for her predecessor to die.

Ava had thought Marc was that special man of her dreams, but within a few weeks of living with him she had come to see a happy future would never be realised with him. He was too much of a playboy, a man who was used to having what he wanted, when he wanted. He was driven to succeed. She had never met a more driven man. He worked hard and he played hard. She had become a part of that play time, but only a very small part and she knew, just like all the other women he had been involved with, her days had been numbered. She had cut the countdown by leaving him, hoping it would protect her from further hurt, not realising how it had played right into the enemy's hands...

'Have you decided what you would like to eat?' Marc asked.

Ava placed her hands in her lap, twisting them together to stop them from shaking. 'I'm not all that hungry,' she said.

He lifted one of his brows. 'Dieting?'

She gave him a resentful look. 'No. I am angry at how you have orchestrated this... this situation.'

His eyes continued to tether hers. 'I am the one who has the right to be angry, Ava, not you. You betrayed me, remember?'

Ava's hands tightened in her lap. She hated thinking of how she had been manipulated into destroying him. How could she have not seen it? It had been a masterful set-up and she had stepped up to the noose without suspecting a thing until it was too late. How could she tell him how blind she had been? He would think she was trying to wriggle out of what she had done by playing the innocent victim. 'It wouldn't matter what I said. You're never going to believe me, are you?' she said.

His jaw ticked. 'I am not going to let you make a fool of me again,' he said. 'This time around I will have my eyes trained on you at all times and in all places.'

Ava stiffened. 'What does that mean? Are you're going to have me followed?'

His expression was inscrutable. 'Fool me once, shame on you, fool me twice, shame on me. Let's say I am taking the necessary steps to keep what is mine exclusively mine this time around.'

She glared at him. 'Women are not possessions you can own, Marc, or at least not in this century.'

He gave a lift of one shoulder as if he couldn't care less what she thought. 'If you are not going to eat then you can watch me, as I am starving,' he said, signalling for the waiter.

'No doubt all the machinations you've been engineering have worked up quite some appetite,' she put in spitefully.

His eyes glinted as he laid the menu to one side. 'Not just for food, *ma belle*,' he said. 'I have other appetites that require satiation, but I am prepared to delay gratification, for a little while at least.'

Ava narrowed her eyes in wariness. 'What do you mean by that?'

He gave her an enigmatic slant of his lips that was almost a smile. 'You think I am such an animal that I would insist on you sleeping with me from day one?'

She pursed her mouth, thinking about it for a moment. 'You're paying me a lot of money,' she said at last. 'I am not sure why you would want to wait on your return on it unless you have a specific agenda in mind.'

'I have no agenda other than the one I stated earlier,' he said. 'I want you to be my temporary mistress. It's as simple as that.'

The waiter approached, which meant Ava had no chance to respond. She gave the man her simple order, while her mind shuffled through various scenarios.

Marc was a proud and bitter man who wanted revenge for the way she had supposedly betrayed him. He had gone to extraordinary lengths to get her back into his life, but it seemed he was not going to rush her into his bed.

Why?

She chewed at her lip as she heard him interact with the waiter, her eyes watching his mouth, the way it moved with each word he articulated. His lips were beautifully sculptured, the lower one fuller than the top one, hinting at the sensuality she had already experienced. Her mouth tingled at the memory of the pressure of his, the way his tongue had played with hers, teasing it, taming it and mating with it until she had melted in his arms.

Marc looked across the table and met her eyes, a hot spurt of lust shooting through his groin as he saw the way her small white teeth were playing with her soft lips. She released her lower lip and the blood flowed back into it, making him want to crush his mouth to hers to taste her beguiling sweetness. Her grey-blue gaze wavered for a moment under the scrutiny of his, her guilt no doubt making her lower it in shame.

His gut twisted with knots of tension as he thought of the photographs in the Press of her wedding to Cole. She had been a beautiful bride; he had never seen a more stunning one, which had somehow made it so much worse. He fisted his hands beneath the table, not trusting himself to hold his wine glass without breaking it. Hardly a day went past when those images didn't taunt him with her perfidy. What a fool he had been to trust her the way he had. He had thought she was playing a game when she left him. He had bided his time, waiting for her to come crawling back to him, begging him to take her back as his mistress. But instead she had humiliated him in the most devastating way possible.

But he was five years older now, five years wiser and five years more successful and powerful. This time things would be different. Ava McGuire had humiliated him before, but this time around he was going to have her right where he wanted her.

Not with his ring on her finger, not even in the palm of his hand, but in his bed for as long as he wanted her.

CHAPTER THREE

ONCE their meals arrived, Ava picked at her salad, her stomach recoiling from every mouthful she tried to swallow. She was intensely aware of Marc's brooding gaze, the ruthless set to his mouth at times unnerved her far more than the sexual tension she could feel pulsing between them.

They had moved to the coffee stage when Ava became aware of a slight commotion behind her. She turned in her seat to see a photographer with his lens aimed at her sitting with Marc.

'Act as naturally as possible,' Marc said in an undertone as he reached for her hand across the table.

Ava felt the blood rush to her fingertips where his fingers touched hers, but she forced her stiff posture to relax, reminding herself all of this was for Serena's sake.

Several photos were taken and the young female journalist who had come in with the photographer asked Marc about his decision to reunite with his ex-mistress.

'Signor Castellano, earlier this evening you released a Press statement citing your intention to resume your relationship with Ava McGuire, the woman who left you for the late property tycoon Douglas Cole five years ago. Do you have anything further to add to that statement?'

Marc gave his white slash of a smile. 'As you can see, we are back together and very happy,' he said. 'That is all I am prepared to say.'

The journalist scribbled madly before asking with a provocative smile, 'Is there any chance of wedding bells in the not too distant future?'

Marc's polite smile was still in place, but Ava could see the flint-like momentary flash in his gaze as it briefly met hers before returning to the journalist's. 'My stance on this subject has not changed. I have no intention of marrying anyone.'

The journalist turned to Ava. 'Mrs Cole, you have developed quite a reputation throughout Europe as a trophy wife. After all, your late husband was thirty-eight years older than you. Do you have any comment to make on that?'

Ava felt Marc's fingers subtly tighten around hers. 'Um…I am not prepared to comment on my private life,' she said, feeling her cheeks flame at the condescending look the journalist was giving her. 'It has always been, and will always remain, off limits.'

The journalist was undaunted. 'Do you have any intention of working for a living other than as Signor Castellano's mistress?'

Ava squared her shoulders. 'I am his…' she paused as she hunted for a word '…his—er—partner, not his mistress.'

The journalist lifted one finely plucked eyebrow. 'His lover, don't you mean?'

Ava felt another warning squeeze from Marc's strong fingers. 'I have already told you I am not prepared to discuss my private life,' she said.

Still with her hand encased in his, Marc rose to his feet, signalling to the journalist that the impromptu interview was now at an end. 'If you will excuse us,' he gave the young woman another smile, 'Miss McGuire and I have a lot of time to catch up on.'

'One last question, Signor Castellano,' the

young woman said as she strategically blocked their exit. 'Does your reunion with Mrs…I mean, Miss McGuire mean you have forgiven her for marrying the man who won the bid for the Dubai hotel over yours? Word has it the contract was as good as yours until she shifted camps, so to speak.'

There was a stiff silence broken only by the clatter of plates and cutlery being cleared from the other tables in the restaurant.

Ava felt every slow-beating second like a hammer blow inside her chest. Her palm was moist and clammy within the cool, dry protection of Marc's hand, her stomach rolling like an out-of-control butter churn. Every breath she took was laboured, as if it had to travel the length of her body to inflate her lungs.

Marc's mouth tightened fractionally. 'But of course,' he said finally. 'The past is in the past. It is time to move on.'

This time the journalist had no choice but to step aside as Marc strode forward with Ava's hand still firmly gripped in his.

It was only once they were in the street outside that his hold loosened, but not enough to release her. The limousine purred to a halt in front of the restaurant entrance like a sleek black panther, its low growl as the driver opened the door for them making Ava feel as if she was stepping into the jaws of a predatory beast to be taken back to its lair and consumed at leisure.

She waited until they were on their way before she turned in her seat to face Marc. 'Did you mean what you said back there or was that just all part of the act for the sake of the public?'

His eyes held hers for a moment before he answered. 'What is done cannot be undone. I am prepared to drop it. It is of no significance to our relationship now.'

Ava screwed up her forehead in a frown. 'No significance?' she asked incredulously. 'How can you say that? Of course it's significant! You don't trust me. But then you never did, did you?'

His broad shoulders visibly stiffened as he held her look, although his expression remained coolly detached. 'I was in lust with you, Ava,' he said. 'From the moment I met you I wanted you. I foolishly let those feelings distract me. I will not make the same mistake again.'

Ava pressed her lips flat and turned to look out of the window at the twinkling lights of the port. His cold, cruel words were like poison darts in her skin, making her wince in pain as each one had hit its mark.

'Why didn't you and Cole have children?' Marc asked after another tense silence.

'It was not what I wanted from him.' Ava cringed as soon as she realised how it sounded, or at least how Marc had interpreted it. She could see the disgust in his eyes, and the way his mouth thinned until it was almost bloodless. 'I mean…it was not on the agenda,' she quickly amended. 'It wasn't something either of us wanted. It wouldn't have suited our…our relationship.'

'What sort of relationship did you have?' Marc asked, using his fingers as quotation marks over the word *relationship*.

Ava felt cornered. She shifted on the leather seat, crossing and uncrossing her legs, her eyes darting away from the steely probe of his. It would be so easy to tell him the truth. That Serena, whilst working for Douglas in his accounts department, had made a series of errors that had meant thousands of pounds had gone missing. Just days after Ava had left Marc, Douglas had threatened Serena with legal action. He had mentioned prison and named a high-profile legal firm who would act for him to ensure Serena would not get away with it. Ava had gone and pleaded on her sister's behalf and a deal had been struck. As distasteful as it was, Ava had accepted the terms, and, although the Press had savaged her time and time again, she bore it with the assurance that she was doing the right thing for Serena—a marriage of convenience for her sister's freedom.

Ava had married a dying man who wanted a fake wife to fool his business associates that he still had it in him to attract a nubile mate. She had hated him for the first four years. She had loathed every minute, biding her time until the missing money was repaid through her role as his wife. But as his illness had finally taken hold she had come to see him not so much as a ruthless businessman, but as a lonely man who, as his life drew to a close, began to recognise the mistakes he had made, most particularly to do with his first wife and two children who no longer had anything to do with him.

Ava forced her gaze to meet Marc's. 'We were…friends.'

Marc threw back his head and laughed.

Ava scowled at him. 'Only someone with your sort of sex-obsessed mind would think like that.'

His arm stretched out on the back of the seat, his fingers so close to the nape of her neck Ava could feel her skin tingling in anticipation for his touch. 'Come now, Ava, don't take me for a fool,' he chided. 'You shared his villa for five years. Do you really expect me to believe you didn't share his bed during some, if not all of that time?'

She lifted her chin, her eyes glittering with hatred. 'I can't control what you think any more than I can control what the Press has reported from time to time. Yes, we shared the villa and, in time, a friendship that was very important to me as it was to him.'

'Were you in love with him?'

Ava eyeballed him. 'No, I was not in love with him, but that's exactly what you expected me to say, wasn't it? You have me pegged as a gold-digger and gold-diggers only love one thing—money, right?'

'You said it, baby,' he said as his fingers became entwined in her hair.

Ava felt a shiver cascade like a trickling fountain down her spine as he drew her closer, inch by inch, until she was almost on his lap. She pushed against his broad chest, straining to get away, but her hair had tethered her to him far more effectively than chains of steel. 'L-let me go,' she said, trying to keep the edge of desperation out of her voice.

'Is that what you really want?' he asked, his warm, coffee-scented breath skating over her lips.

Her eyelids lowered, her tongue coming out to brush over her lips to moisten them as her chest rose and fell in rising panic. 'Don't do this, Marc…not yet…I'm not ready…'

'Not quite ready to beg?' he asked, brushing the pad of his thumb where her tongue had just been.

She watched in a spellbound stasis as he ran his own tongue over the end of his thumb, tasting her. It was such an intimate act, it made her stomach hollow out and her legs weaken, the base of her spine melting into a pool, like honey poured from a hot jug. Her mouth prickled with the need to feel his hard mouth on hers, to feel the thrust and glide of his masterful tongue claiming hers, taming it into submission.

'It's all right,' he said, releasing her hair and moving back along the seat. 'I can wait until you are ready.'

Ava felt herself slump like a sack of wet washing without his support. She ran an agitated hand through her hair, hating him for being so in control when she was so undone by his very presence, let alone his touch. Every hair on her head seemed to be crying out for the sensual comb of his fingers. Her heart was still thumping inside her chest wall, the exquisite expectation of his kiss and then the sudden let-down was too much for her to have any chance of regulating her pulse.

It was a revelation to her that even after all this time and all the bitterness she had stored in her heart against him, he could still turn her into a helpless pool of need. She was ashamed of her weakness, knowing how it would please him no end to be aware of it as he surely must be, if not already, then as time went on as they shared the villa according to his arrangements.

Think of the money, think of Serena, she chanted to herself. She silently garnered her courage, steeling her resolve to keep her heart intact this time around. He could do what he liked, treat her like the wanton woman he thought she was, but this time he was not going to break her heart the way he had done before. She would be his mistress, she could act both in public and in private, but he was not going to have the one part of her that she had so freely given him before.

The driver pulled into the driveway of the villa, the gates swinging open via the remote security device as the car's wheels growled along the gravel to come to a halt outside the stately entrance.

Marc helped Ava from the car and escorted her up the stone steps to the massive foyer. The scent of the fresh roses Celeste had arranged on the marble hall table earlier filled the air, somehow giving the commodious residence a homely feel. Ava had done what she could over the last few months of Douglas's life to make the place as comfortable and peaceful as she could. She had always found the austere formality of the villa offputting, and over the years she had lived there had made some subtle changes that had made her feel less intimidated.

The removal men had been busy while Ava and Marc were at dinner, for upon entering the formal sitting room she could see various works of art belonging to Marc already hanging on the walls. It was as if he was marking his territory. Even when she excused herself to use the bathroom upstairs she saw that he had taken over the master bedroom. Two well-travelled suitcases lay open on the bed as well as a black toiletries bag. Even the air smelled of him, that enticing aroma of citrus and male phero-mones that never failed to make her toes curl.

'Madame?' Celeste appeared from the walk-in wardrobe. 'Did you want me for something?'

'Non, Celeste,' Ava said, blushing at being caught peering into Marc's domain. 'I was just…er…checking that Signor Castellano has everything he needs.'

'Oui,' Celeste said. 'I was given instruc-tions to unpack for him.' She seemed to hesitate before asking, 'Shall I move your things in here too?'

Ava's eyes rounded, her heart banging against her breastbone like a church bell pulled too hard. 'Did he ask you to do that?'

Celeste gave a Gallic shrug. 'It is in-evitable, *oui*?'

Ava pulled her shoulders back. 'What makes you say that?'

'He is a very handsome man,' Celeste said as if that explained everything.

Ava pursed her lips, wondering how to explain the situation. 'Look, Celeste,' she began, 'I don't want you to think the wrong thing, but—'

'It is all right, *madame*,' Celeste assured her with a knowing look. 'I was young once. You have a history with him, *oui*? It is hard to resist a man who has gone to such trouble to get you back in his life.'

Ava frowned. 'Celeste…I'm not sure you understand. Marc Castellano ruined Douglas. He took everything off him. His ex-wife was left with nothing, not to mention his children. Douglas wanted Adam and Lucy to have something to remember him by. It was his dying wish.'

Celeste glanced past Ava's shoulder, clearing her throat diplomatically. '*Excusez-moi, Signor Castellano*,' she said with a little bow. 'I am not quite finished unpacking your things.'

'*C'est bien, Celeste. Je vais me reposer*,' he said. '*Bonsoir.*'

'*Bonsoir*,' Celeste said and exchanging a conspiratorial raised-brow look with Ava on the way past, left to make her way downstairs.

'Do you have any objections to my taking over this room?' Marc asked.

'No objections at all,' Ava answered in an

offhand, couldn't-care-less tone. 'The villa belongs to you. You can sleep where you like.'

His dark eyes contained a hint of amusement as they meshed with hers. 'Is that an invitation to join you in your bed?'

She crossed her arms, her mouth flattening with reproach. 'No, it is not.'

He lifted a hand to her face, trailing his fingertips down the curve of her cheek, his touch stirring every nerve to zinging life. He stopped just short of her mouth, his index finger touching the tiny crease at the corner that so rarely these days lifted upwards in a smile. Ava held her breath, feeling her whole body sway towards him. It was like a magnetic force pulling her towards him. She lowered her lashes to avoid his gaze, but he countered it by placing a fingertip beneath her chin, pinning her gaze with his.

'I was surprised to find you weren't occupying the master suite,' he said. 'When did you move out of your husband's bed?'

Ava felt her breath tighten in her throat. Should she tell him she had never occupied it? Would he believe her? No, of course not, she thought. Given the way Douglas had insisted they give every appearance of a normal relationship in public, it would take more than a few words from her to counter the many Press photographs that had been printed with Douglas's arm around her waist or gazing at her adoringly. It had sickened her to be complicit in the web of lies that surrounded their relationship, but it had saved Serena and that was all Ava really cared about. 'He was very ill towards the end,' she said. 'But in any case, we decided early on to have separate rooms. He wasn't a good sleeper. He…he had terrible insomnia.'

Marc moved away from her and, picking up a silver-framed photograph of Serena and Richard's wedding day, examined it for a moment or two before placing it back down. He turned back to face her, his expression mask-like. 'What did your sister have to say about your relationship with Cole?'

Ava tried to keep her expression as blank as possible. 'Serena was the one who introduced me to him in the first place,' she said. 'She worked in the accounts department in his London office.'

'So it was a whirlwind affair.' It was neither a statement nor a question, so Ava didn't respond. Silence seemed so much safer—fewer lies to tell that she might regret later.

He glanced at the wedding photograph again before returning his gaze to hers. 'Your sister lives a very different life from what you have chosen for yourself. And yet you are still very close, are you not?'

'We have our moments like any sisters do,' Ava answered. 'Since our mother died when I was nine, Serena, being two years younger, has always looked up to me as a mother. But you know all this. I told you about it when we met five years ago.'

He studied her for an endless pause, his eyes roving hers as if searching for something deep inside them. 'Yes, you did,' he finally said. 'I told you how I envied you, remember? Being an only child left me with many burdens to carry alone.'

Ava remembered well how deeply Marc's childhood had affected him. Whenever he had spoken of it, which was rarely, she got a sense of the acute loneliness of him as a young, bewildered little boy with no one to turn to for comfort. In the beginning she had hoped to be the one to heal him of his childhood wounds by loving him and cherishing him for the rest of their lives. Somehow it seemed all the more tragic now that he was likely to spend the rest of his life moving from one pointless relationship to the other, never trusting or loving someone long enough to build a lifetime together.

'I have to go to London early next week,' Marc said. 'I would like you to come with me. It will give you a chance to catch up with your sister.'

Ava's forehead creased again. Serena would take one look at her with Marc and realise something was up. 'But I've just come back from London,' she said. 'I've barely unpacked.'

'I am sure your sister will be delighted to see you again so soon,' he said.

Ava pressed her lips together, dropping her gaze from his. 'Serena hasn't been well just lately,' she said, twisting her hands together. 'I don't think now is the right time for her to have visitors.'

'I am sorry to hear that. Is it something serious?'

Ava lifted her gaze back to his. 'She has had several miscarriages over the last couple of years,' she said. 'The last one was at four months along, just ten days ago. It was very traumatic for her, as you can imagine.'

His dark eyes showed his compassion, which made it all the harder for Ava to summon up her ill feelings towards him. It reminded her of how tender he had been with her in the past whenever the slightest ailment had struck her. How she had longed for such tenderness over the last five years!

'I am very sorry,' he said deeply. 'The loss must be truly devastating for both your sister and her husband. But would not another visit from you be just what she needs to cheer her up?'

Ava crossed her arms over her chest again, hoping it would ease the tight ache of her heart. 'I am not sure… She was not up to visitors while I was there. I can call Richard and see what he thinks, but I don't think he'll be too happy about it. They both are suffering terribly. It's been a huge disappointment.'

'Ava, it is important that we are seen together as a couple, not just here in Monte Carlo, but also when I have to travel elsewhere for business,' Marc said in a serious tone.

She raised her brows at him cynically. 'What you mean is you want me under lock and key so you can control every move I make, don't you, Marc?'

He worked his jaw for a moment, as if trying to withhold a stinging retort. 'I am paying you to be my mistress, Ava,' he said after a small, tense pause. 'It is part of the job description. After all, you accompanied Douglas Cole whenever he travelled abroad, hanging off his arm like a limpet.'

'That was different,' Ava said without thinking.

He lifted one dark brow in a perfect arc. 'How so?'

She compressed her lips, lowering her eyes again. 'Douglas was very ill in the last few months of his life,' she said. 'He needed more and more support from me in order to travel for business.'

'I bet you hated every minute of tending to his needs,' Marc said. 'It is not quite the role you were expecting when you accepted the role as his bride, now, was it? But then the lure of the money would be enough to induce you to do anything, would it not?'

She gave him a cutting glare and turned her back to him. 'I hope you are not expecting me to mop your sweaty brow for you some time in the future, for I won't do it.'

Marc felt his hands tense and forced each of his fingers to unclench. Her defiance both irritated and aroused him. She was much feistier than she had been in the past, but then the sweet, loving woman he had thought he had known back then had all been an act, an artful, devious disguise to get him to take his focus off his business so she could undercut him with her partnership with Cole. This was the real Ava McGuire: tough, combative and furious at him for having her under his thumb at last. He was going to enjoy every minute of taming her. They would be dynamite in bed together, perhaps even more so than they had been before. He could feel the electric tightness of the air whenever she came near him; her body gave off pulsing waves of attraction that ran over his skin, heating it to boiling point. It was all he could do not to push her up against the nearest wall and take her roughly any way he could, satisfying this aching, burning need that throbbed incessantly in his groin. He could feel it now, the burgeoning of his flesh, the rush of blood that made him swell with longing.

'I promise you I will not ask you to mop my brow, *cara*,' he said, watching as she shook the waves of her blonde hair back past her shoulders as if its length annoyed her. 'I have other places on my body I would much rather you pay close attention to.'

She swung back to face him, her grey-blue

eyes flashing silver daggers at him. 'You think you can make me do anything you want, don't you?' she asked. 'But I am no man's plaything. I have never been and never will be.'

'Ah, but that is not true, now, is it, *ma petite*?' Marc asked as he came closer again, taking her by the shoulders this time. 'Cole got to play with you all he liked. Now it is my turn.'

Her slim throat moved up and down, the tension in her shoulders palpable under the gentle but firm pressure of his hands. 'I've changed my mind,' she said, eyeballing him determinedly. 'I want double the money.'

He lifted a single brow at her calculating behaviour. 'We agreed on a price, Ava. I am not paying you more than you are worth, especially since you are what one would call "used goods".'

Her mouth tightened, but to his surprise her chin gave a tiny wobble before she got it back under control. She blinked at him a couple of times, which made him wonder if she was close to tears.

A trick or a tactic? He couldn't quite make up his mind. Instead he did what he had longed to do from the moment he had turned up at the villa earlier that evening.

He bent his head and, before she could do anything to counteract it, he lowered his mouth to hers.

Ava had no time to prepare herself for his kiss, not that she could have even if she'd had a lifetime or two. The passion that roared between their mouths was like an inferno as soon as contact was made. Her lips throbbed and burned and blistered with longing as his ground against hers, roughly at first, angrily almost, as if he hated himself for still wanting her. She kissed him back with equal rage; annoyed at how she still wanted him, how she had wanted him to kiss her as if the last five years hadn't happened.

The pressure of his mouth on hers grew and grew until with just one stabbing thrust of his tongue she opened to him, her whole body melting in his rough hold, her spine almost collapsing, throwing her forward so his arms had to leave her shoulders to wrap around her body instead, holding her up against his rock-hard form. She felt every delicious arrantly male inch of him, the way his erection pounded against her belly, reminding her of how powerfully he was made, and how explosive he could be in the final moments of release.

His tongue explored her mouth in intimate detail, shockingly intimate: licking, sucking and stroking until she was whimpering in response. His teeth nipped at the fullness of her lower lip, fuelling her desire to an unmanageable, uncontrollable level. She gasped as he moved from her mouth to run his tongue over the sensitive skin of her neck before he used his teeth on her, pulling at her flesh teasingly, taunting her to play the same dangerous game with him.

Ava put her lips to the stubbly skin of his neck, shivering in response as his peppered skin rasped against the softness of her lips, relishing in that exquisite reminder of how male he was and how softly feminine she was in comparison. He tasted of citrus and salt and a hint of male sweat, a tantalising cocktail that had her head spinning faster than any triple-strength Cosmopolitan could ever do.

She used her tongue like a cat, licking him softly at first, tentatively, teasing him until he growled deep in his throat. She bit him then, a soft, playful little nip that tugged at his skin, making him press himself against her pelvis with throbbing urgency as his need for her grew thick and hard and insistent.

She rubbed against him wantonly as she went for his neck again, harder this time, her spine turning to molten wax as he swore roughly and returned to her mouth, covering it with his with almost bruising strength. Ava tasted blood, but she wasn't sure if it was hers or his. She didn't care, all she could think about was having this kiss go on and on, to be held like this, so firmly, so possessively and so passionately. It had been so long since she had felt this exhilarating sense of abandonment. Her body felt as if it had come to life again after being shut down for five lonely years. Every drop of her blood raced through her veins, every nerve-ending bloomed and buzzed with feeling and every pore of her skin ached to feel him touch her intimately.

She felt his hands glide over her breasts beneath her top, cupping them through her lacy bra, before he deftly released its clasp at the back to hold her skin on skin. The palms of his hands were warm and slightly rough, again a delicious reminder of how intensely male he was. She quivered as he gently pinched her nipples, rolling them between his finger and thumb until they were hard as pebbles and achingly sensitive.

Ava drew in a scratchy breath as he lowered his mouth to her right breast, taking her in his mouth, the hot moistness anointing her, ramping up her need for him until she was almost gibbering with desire.

'Please…oh, please…' she groaned as he moved to her other breast.

She felt him smile around her nipple, as if her reaction to him pleased him no end. She shuddered as he suckled on her hungrily, his mouth a sweet torture on her senses. She arched backwards, gasping for air, for release, for the pleasure only he could deliver.

'Marc…please…*please*…'

He lifted his mouth off her breast and met her feverish gaze. His eyes glinted with satisfaction, his mouth tilting in mocking amusement. 'Look at how easy you are for the taking,' he said. 'One kiss and I could have had you right here and right now.'

Ava had never slapped anyone in her life; she abhorred violence of any sort, but her hand went flying through the air towards his face before she could stop it. Luckily he did. He captured her wrist, halting its progress.

'Violence is not and will not be a part of this relationship,' he said with gravitas.

Ava raised her chin, not even bothering to blink back her tears. 'You started it.' She flung at him accusingly. 'You were too rough.'

His eyes went to her mouth. She saw the shock register in his gaze, the sudden flare of his eyes as they saw the tiny split she could feel on her lower lip. 'Forgive me. I was too rough with you. It will not happen again.'

Ava wanted it to happen again. She wanted him to lose control so she would not be the only one suffering this empty, unfulfilled ache deep inside. She also wanted him in this mood, this tender, concerned Marc she had once or twice caught a glimpse of in the past. Fresh tears came to her eyes, cascading down her cheeks unheeded as she stood before him, her heart contracting painfully for how she had loved and lost him.

Marc's brows drew together. 'Does it hurt *that* much, *cara*?' he asked gently.

Ava wrenched out of his hold with unnecessary force considering he was barely touching her, let alone restraining her in any way. 'It's not about my lip, damn you,' she threw at him, angry at herself for losing control in front of him.

He silently handed her a clean, neatly

folded and pressed white handkerchief, his eyes intensely dark and watchful as they held hers.

Ava took the square of fabric with a hand that was a little unsteady, and gently dabbed at her mouth, conscious of him studying her every movement. She scrunched up the handkerchief after she had finished, but when he reached for it she held it behind her back. 'No,' she said. 'It'll need soaking. I'll see to it.'

'You don't need to do that,' he said with a wry look. 'You can throw it away or give it to the household staff to clean. I am not expecting you to do my laundry, Ava.'

Ava kept the handkerchief tightly clutched in her hand. She had smelled his clean male scent on it as she'd held it to her mouth. She wasn't going to give it back, she decided. If it was the only thing she had left of him when this was over then so be it.

'I would like to go to bed,' she said in a subdued tone as she felt the fight go out of her. 'I'm very tired.'

Marc stepped back and held the door open for her. 'I will bring you a nightcap once you are in bed. What about a little brandy in milk?'

She shook her head, the movement making

her fragrant hair swing around her shoulders, making him ache to thread his fingers through the soft, silky strands. 'No, thank you,' she said a little stiffly as she moved past him.

'Ava?'

She froze mid-step; her slim back rigid, reminding him of a small ironing board standing upright. 'Please, Marc…not now. I just couldn't bear it.'

Marc drew in a breath that snagged at his throat as she continued on her way down the wide hall, disappearing into a suite several doors down.

Tears or a tactic? he asked himself again. But he was no closer to the truth. If anything, he thought he was even further away.

The following morning when Ava finally made it downstairs, Celeste handed her the phone. 'It is your sister, Serena,' she said, covering the mouthpiece with her hand.

Ava took the phone and wandered out to the terrace rather than have the housekeeper or indeed Marc overhear her conversation. 'Serena?' she said once she was out of earshot. 'How are you, sweetie?'

'Is it true?' Serena asked without

preamble, her voice breathless with shock. 'Are you really living with Marc Castellano as his mistress?'

Ava took a deep but uneven breath. 'Serena…I was going to call you to explain, but it got late last night and I—'

'What's going on?' Serena asked. 'For all this time you've never mentioned his name. I thought you hated him. You told me it was over between you, that you would never go back to him.'

Ava knew she had to tread carefully with how much she told her sister. In accepting Douglas Cole's marriage proposal, she had pretended her feelings for Marc had been obliterated by his refusal to commit. She hadn't wanted Serena to feel any more guilt than she had at the time. To reveal Marc's motives for their reconciliation would cause unnecessary hurt to Serena when she already had enough pain to deal with over the loss of her baby. 'Serena, it's sort of complicated…' she began.

'Have you slept with him?'

Ava rolled her lips together, wincing as she felt the slight swelling of her lower lip. 'No,' she said on an expelled breath. 'Not yet.'

'So what's going on?' Serena asked again, her voice going an octave higher. 'It's in every paper over here. They all say the same thing—that you've reconciled with Marc. It even says here…' there was a rustling of pages being turned '…that he now owns Douglas's villa and his company. Everything! He owns the lot.'

'Yes, that's true,' Ava said, swallowing tightly.

'How long have you known about this?'

'Er—not long.'

'Ava?' Serena's voice cracked. 'This is all my fault, isn't it? If I hadn't been so stupid to make those mistakes in the books none of this would have happened. I feel so guilty. Don't think I don't realise you gave up five years of your life for me. I know you've always said you enjoyed being married to Douglas because of the money and the lifestyle but I never really believed it. You're not that type of person in spite of what the Press likes to think. Oh, God, I can't bear to think of Marc trying to get back at you for—'

'No,' Ava said firmly. 'None of this has anything to do with you and the past.' She mentally crossed her fingers at her little white lie and added, 'Marc still has—er—

feelings for me. He's waited this long for the chance to come back into my life. We are both keen to have another go at our relationship. We were young and headstrong before. We've both moved on.'

'So…what about your feelings about him?' Serena asked after a short silence. 'Are you saying you were in love with him all this time?'

Ava pinched the bridge of her nose. 'It's hard to know what I feel right now,' she said, carefully sidestepping her sister's question. 'I just want to enjoy getting to know him again. We're taking things slowly this time.'

'Has he changed his mind about marriage and kids?' Serena asked.

Ava felt a pain deep inside her heart, like a toothpick being twisted. 'It's a bit of a touchy subject.'

'Ava, don't waste any more years of your life, please, I beg you,' Serena said, starting to cry. 'You deserve a happy life. You've already sacrificed so much…'

There was the sound of someone in the background and then suddenly a male voice came on the line. 'Ava? Is that you?' Richard Holt said in his crisp Cambridge-educated voice.

'Yes,' Ava answered. 'Richard, I'm so sorry, I didn't mean to upset Serena but—'

'It's all right,' Richard sighed long-sufferingly. 'She's been through a bad patch just lately, poor little pet. The doctors say it's the hormones, you know…after…well…' he cleared his throat '…you know.'

Ava felt her own throat thicken with emotion for what they were both going through. 'I understand, Richard,' she said softly. 'I am *so* sorry for not breaking the news of my reunion with Marc to you both personally. It's just everything's been happening so quickly and I…well…I'm sorry. You and Serena should have been the first to know, not read about it in the Press as you did.'

'We are thrilled for you, really we are,' Richard said with genuine warmth. 'Don't pay any attention to Serena just now. She's not herself. Once she realises you are happy she'll be absolutely tickled pink for you.'

There was a tiny pause before he added, 'Erm…you are happy, aren't you, my dear?'

Ava forced her voice to sound light and carefree. 'I am happy, Richard. Marc and I are like different people now. It's a fresh start.'

'That's wonderful,' he said. 'Absolutely brilliant news. Bring him over to see us as soon as you can so we can toast your future.'

Ava grimaced. 'I'll do that.'

Ava hung up the phone a short time later just as Marc stepped out onto the terrace. She tucked a strand of her hair behind one ear with her free hand, feeling colour creep like a slow-moving tide along her cheeks.

'Your sister?' he asked, glancing at the phone in her other hand.

She nodded and, looking at the phone, put it down on the outdoor table, carefully avoiding his gaze. 'And my brother-in-law.' She gave a little sigh. 'They read about—er—us…in the papers.'

His steps sounded on the tiles of the terrace as he came to stand in a short distance in front of her. 'I should have suggested you call them last night.'

Ava glanced up at him. 'I should have thought of it myself.'

He came a step closer and gently lifted her chin with two of his fingers as his dark, fathomless gaze studied her mouth for an endless moment. 'Your lip is swollen,' he said with a gruffness she had not heard him use before. 'I should have brought you some ice to put on it last night.'

Ava stepped out of his hold, frightened she would betray herself by leaning into his solid warmth. 'I'm perfectly fine,' she said, injecting a tart quality into her voice. 'I need coffee, not first aid.'

'I have already instructed Celeste to bring it out to us here,' he said. 'You look like you could do with some sunshine. You look rather pale this morning.'

'I didn't sleep well,' Ava confessed, glancing up at him again as he pulled a chair out for her at the outdoor table setting.

'Not used to sleeping alone?' he asked with a wry lift of one dark brow.

She gave him a look that would have sliced through frozen butter. 'You just can't help yourself, can you, Marc?'

He pulled out a chair for himself and sat down, waiting until Celeste had brought out a tray with coffee and fresh croissants and preserve, and left them alone again, before he spoke. 'Why didn't you tell me you never shared a bed with Cole the whole time you were married?'

Ava stared at him for a moment, dumb-struck at the out-of-the-blue question.

'How…?' She swallowed and began again, 'How do you know?'

He nodded in the direction Celeste had gone. 'The housekeeper let it slip.'

Ava shifted in her chair. 'I'm surprised you believed her,' she said, throwing him a stinging look. 'If I had told you, I am sure you would have laughed in my face.'

A camera shutter-quick movement came and went in his gaze as it held hers. 'I guess I should take some comfort in the knowledge you married him solely for the money,' he said. 'After all, you never complained about our sex life while we were together.'

Ava felt her body quiver in remembrance and quickly shifted her gaze from the probe of his. Her shoulders went back until they met the sun-warmed wrought-iron lace of her chair, twin pools of heat burning in her cheeks.

She watched as he poured them both a coffee, his movements so steady and sure, while her body was trembling both inside and out. She swallowed a tight knot of tension in her throat, wondering how to fill the chasm of silence that had opened up between them.

Marc handed her a cup of steaming coffee,

his eyes meeting hers across the small distance of the round table. 'I could have given you as much, if not more than Cole, so why did you do it?'

She took the cup from him, the slight rattle of it in its saucer betraying her outwardly cool composure. 'You refused to give me what I wanted,' she said. 'If I had stayed with you I would never have been a bride. Douglas at least allowed me to experience that.'

Marc felt the familiar punch of jealousy hit him in the midsection when he thought of her as a bride. Even knowing the marriage had not been consummated barely lessened its impact. For all he knew she could have taken any number of lovers during her marriage, after all, Cole had been very ill before he died. Perhaps his health had been impaired much longer than the public had been aware of. But when all was said and done, Ava had still ditched Marc to enter into a paper marriage to his enemy to bring about his ruin. What other reason could she have had?

He rested his right ankle over his left thigh, leaning back in his chair as he idly stirred his coffee with a silver-crested spoon that had been in his family for hundreds of years. It occurred to him then that once he died there would be no Castellano heir to inherit that and every other heirloom his father's family had collected over the years. Marc had fought so hard to keep every last object in his possession when his business had almost gone under. If he didn't have an heir when he died everything would have to go to another branch of the family, distant cousins Marc barely knew. He had never really thought about it until now. How it would feel to have no one to pass on the family name. The proud heritage he had built up almost from scratch when his father had toppled emotionally would be lost forever.

He pinned her gaze with his. 'Why is marriage such a big thing for you? It's little more than a piece of paper, or at least apparently it was in your case with Cole.'

'There were good reasons why that was the case,' she said, lowering her eyes. 'Douglas was unable to…to—'

'To get it up?' he offered.

Her eyes flicked back to his, irritation flashing in their grey-blue depths. 'Sex is not the only basis for a happy marriage,' she said. 'Illness or an accident can strike anyone at any time. That's the whole point of prom-

ising to love for better or worse, sickness
and health and so on.'

'Were your parents happily married before
your mother died?' he asked.

She averted her gaze once more. 'No, but
that doesn't mean good marriages don't
exist. Even people who are completely different can make a wonderful go of it. My
sister and her husband are a perfect example.
Serena is incredibly shy and Richard is at
ease with people and very outgoing. They
make a lovely couple in every way.'

Marc felt a frown pull at his brow as he sat
watching her. The sunlight on her blonde hair
highlighted its naturalness, the soft waves
framing her face making her look like an
angel. He had missed the sound of her voice.
He hadn't realised until now how much. She
had a softly spoken voice, her fluency with
foreign languages giving her a cultured
accent that was mesmerising to listen to. She
could have read her way through the phone
book and he would have gladly sat and lis-
tened for hours.

He gave himself a mental shake and took
a deep sip of his coffee. 'Perhaps you are
right,' he said. 'But then opposites attract.
Like us, *sì*?'

'You seem more intent on attacking me than attracting me,' she put in with a testy look.

Marc put his cup back down, his mouth tightening at her jibe. The truth was he was deeply ashamed of how he had inadvertently hurt her by kissing her so savagely.

'I don't suppose people will take our reconciliation very seriously if we are forever sniping at each other,' he said, offering her a croissant.

She pushed the basket back towards him. 'No, thank you,' she said. 'I just want coffee for now.'

'You haven't even touched it.'

'I'm waiting for it to cool down.'

'You should eat something,' he said. 'You look thinner than when we were together five years ago.'

She gave him a flinty look. 'Yes, well, after the little strip show you insisted on last night you could probably calculate my weight to the nearest gram.'

Marc suppressed a smile at the memory which had kept him awake for hours last night. He had enjoyed every second of seeing her in just her bra and knickers and he couldn't wait to see her in even less. 'I know it is supposedly fashionable to be bone-thin, but personally I like a little flesh to hold on to,' he said.

She rolled her eyes in disdain. 'If you think I am going to stuff myself full of sugar and fat just to please you then you will be waiting a long time.'

'Are you on the Pill?'

Ava blinked at him, hastily trying to reorient herself before she answered. 'Yes, not that it's any of your business.'

He gave her a smouldering look. 'Soon will be, *cara*. We have a deal, remember?'

Ava crossed her legs and her arms, but even so her body still felt as if it had been set alight with longing. Just thinking about him making love to her made her skin tingle from the base of her spine to the roots of her hair. 'You can hardly force yourself on me,' she pointed out.

He gave her a knowing smile. 'I don't think there will be any chance of that being an issue for two reasons. The first is I do not believe in forcing a woman to have sex with me, and the second is you are just as attracted to me as I am to you. That is one thing that hasn't changed in the five years we have been apart.'

Ava shifted agitatedly in her chair. 'You're imagining it. I hate you. I detest every minute I have to spend with you.'

His mouth curved upwards into a lazy smile. 'Then perhaps the sooner we make love and get it over with the better, *sì*? Who knows? Perhaps I will be bored by you within a week or two.'

'I wish,' she muttered.

He reached across the table and took her wrist in his hand, his fingers overlapping her fragile form, reminding her yet again of how outclassed she was in trying to win a single battle with him, let alone the war. His eyes burned as they held hers, searing her to the core. 'I think it's time you stopped playing games with me, Ava,' he said. 'I know what you are doing. All those little secrets and lies are for a purpose, are they not?'

Ava gritted her teeth as she pulled out of his hold. 'I am not playing any games. If anyone is guilty of that it is you, blackmailing me back into your life the way you have.'

He gave her a contemptuous look as he rose from the table. 'You can leave any minute you wish, Ava,' he said. 'But if you go you will not be taking a penny or a single possession with you. All you will be taking is a folder full of bills your husband left unpaid. Do I make myself clear?'

She sat fuming at him, stubbornly refusing to answer, hating him with such intensity she was practically shaking all over with it.

'I said, do I make myself clear?' he barked at her.

Ava rose to her feet in one stiff, angry movement which toppled her chair backwards onto the terrace tiles. 'Don't you dare raise your voice at me!' she said, glaring at him.

Celeste came running at the sound of the chair crashing to the ground, but Marc sent her away with a look that would have stopped an express train in its tracks.

He turned back to Ava once the housemaid had scuttled away, his eyes still flashing their ire. 'This is not how I wish our relationship to be conducted,' he said, lowering his voice with an obvious effort. 'You will learn respect if I have to spend every hour of every day teaching you.'

Ava curled her top lip at him, even though she knew it was likely to stoke his anger towards her. 'How is our relationship going to be conducted, then?' she asked. 'With you insulting me at every turn, calling me every vilifying name you can think of as if you've never put a foot wrong in your life. Your hypocrisy is nauseating. You've made plenty of mistakes, Marc. The difference is you won't admit to them.'

When she moved past him to leave the terrace Marc let her go without a word. He picked up the lukewarm coffee and took a sip, frowning heavily as he looked at the sparkling blue water of the ocean below.

CHAPTER FOUR

AVA spent the rest of the morning in her room, filling in time by sorting through her wardrobe, a task that she could just as easily have assigned to Celeste, but she wanted the mental space of a menial activity to calm her restive mind.

When she came downstairs for a light lunch Celeste informed her Marc had left the villa and would not be back until dinner. Ava felt her tense shoulders and the tight band around her head instantly relax.

The heat of the day drove Ava out to the infinity pool Douglas had installed in the terraced gardens at the back of the villa. It was one of Ava's favourite spots, for the screen of the shrubs gave her a sense of privacy as she swam lap after lap. The sun was warm, but the water spilling over her with each stroke she took felt like cool silk, the sensual glide of her body through the water making her feel weightless and free.

She wasn't quite sure of when she first realised she was no longer alone. At first it was just a prickling-at-the-back-of-the-neck sensation that she was being watched, but when she stopped at the end of the pool she could see no sign of anyone about. However, it was on her last lap that she noticed Marc sitting on one of the sun loungers, looking magnificently male in nothing but his black close-fitting bathers. Every muscle of his abdomen looked as if it had been carved from dark marble. Not a gram of excess flesh was on him anywhere. She could see he was no stranger to the discipline of regular and hard exercise. If anything, he was looking even fitter and leaner than he had in the past.

'You swim well,' he said, lifting his sunglasses to prop them just above his hairline.

'Thank you,' she said and, using the steps at the side of the pool, came out of the water, trying not to feel self-conscious in her bikini.

She felt Marc's eyes on her as she went to the other sun lounger, where she had left her towel, the heat of his gaze warming her far more than the late-afternoon sun. She used her towel like a sarong around her body before she faced him. 'Celeste told me you weren't coming back to the villa until later this evening.'

He placed his hands behind his head as he stretched out on the lounger, the action making every carved contour of his biceps bulge with latent strength. 'I finished the business I had to see to earlier than expected,' he said.

Ava narrowed her gaze as she stalled in the process of wringing out her wet hair over her shoulder. 'Were you checking up on me by any chance?' she asked.

He crossed his ankles in an indolent manner, his dark eyes still roving her form so thoroughly she felt her skin prickle all over with sensory awareness. 'Were you thinking of an escape route?' he countered.

Ava pursed her lips, letting the damp rope of her hair go. 'Is there one I could use that would succeed?'

He smiled a confident smile. 'No.' He leaned back even farther in the lounger. 'I have thought of everything, *cara*. You have no choice but to stay with me or face the consequences of your late husband's debts.'

Ava tightened her towel around her body. 'If I am to be shackled to you indefinitely I

would like something to do to fill my time,'
she said. 'While I was…' she hesitated ever
so briefly over her choice of word '…living
with Douglas I helped him with some aspects
of the business.'

Marc rose from the lounger, dropping his
sunglasses back over his eyes. 'You can't
have been keeping too close an eye on them,
otherwise you would have seen the way
things were and left him and his sinking ship
long ago,' he remarked.

Ava felt her heart give a little flutter as he
stepped closer. She had no way of escaping
unless she stepped backwards into the pool.
'Th-that's because towards the end when he
became ill I left things to his accountants and
business manager and instead looked after
him myself.'

'Why didn't you leave him while you had
the chance, or didn't he give you a choice?'

'It might surprise you, but yes, he did give
me a choice, but I felt I owed it to him to
stay,' she said. 'He had no one else. He
wasn't close to his children, which he re-
gretted deeply. I felt sorry for him. He didn't
want to die alone.'

Although Ava couldn't see Marc's eyes on
account of his sunglasses, she could feel the

cynicism of his gaze all the same. 'You expect me to believe you personally nursed him?' he asked.

Ava lifted her chin. 'It was the least I could do. After all, he had been very good to me.'

'Oh, yes,' he said with a lift of one side of his mouth. 'He was very good to you indeed. He apparently paid you a minor fortune, didn't he? Where is it now, Ava? Where is all the money he paid you over the years?'

Ava felt a footstep of unease press on the base of her spine. 'That is none of your business,' she said, instinctively stepping backwards, momentarily forgetting the body of water behind her.

She teetered for a nanosecond before Marc took her by the upper arms, his fingers warm and firm against her flesh. Her towel slipped to the pool deck, but Ava hardly noticed; she was far too aware of how close he was to her body and how hers was responding to him as if she had no choice in the matter. Her breasts pushed against her bikini top, the sensitive nipples tight with the ache to feel him touch her. Her hips were within touching distance of his, the temptation to press herself against him and feel his hardness was almost unbearable.

'Large amounts of money have been going from your account to your sister's in London,' Marc said. 'Do you want to tell me what that money was for or should I have someone investigate it for me at the risk of causing embarrassment to your sister or her husband or both?'

She glared up at him with stormy grey-blue eyes. 'How dare you invade my privacy, not to mention my sister's, like that?'

His fingers tightened as she tried to sidestep his hold. Anger was on her side, however, and somehow he misjudged his footwork. With a tangle of limbs Marc found himself falling, taking Ava with him into the open blue mouth of the pool.

She came up spluttering, her arms flailing at him in fury, knocking his sunglasses off in the process. 'You did that on purpose, you… you…beast!'

Marc captured her wrists and pulled her up against his body, his blood surging to his groin as soon as her pelvis rammed against his. Her body felt like silk against his, soft and sensual, her limbs curling around his to keep herself afloat. He took advantage of every sweet moment, relishing in the feel of her mound against the press of his erection.

She was fighting herself rather than him, he realised with an inward smile of satisfaction. He could feel it in the way her body pressed and pushed against him simultaneously, as if she resented what she was feeling but wanted it anyway. In the end he made it easy for her—he bent his head and his mouth swooped down to cover hers, his tongue delving deeply to bring hers to submission.

Within seconds she melted with a sigh, her tongue dancing with his, her arms lacing around his neck as he nudged her to the edge of the pool where it was shallow enough to stand. He stood with his thighs apart, her slim form fitting perfectly against him, her mouth hot and wet and urgent under the heated pressure and exploration of his.

The blood roared in his veins, thundering in his ears until all he could think about was sinking into her slick velvet warmth. He had wanted to wait, to have her begging for him, not the other way around, but his body was on fire with flames of need so intense he could feel them licking at him with long tongues of blistering heat. His whole body throbbed with it, the powerful attraction he had always felt for her seemed to have intensified now he finally had her in his arms. He had never been so close to losing control, or at least not since he was a hormone-charged teenager. The thought of exploding within her, feeling her convulsing around him made his blood sizzle as it raced through him. He ached with the pressure, the need so great he moved against her softness, searching for her, his spine tingling as she responded by whimpering with desire.

Ava felt the tiled lip of the pool at her back as Marc's body pressed against her searchingly, the heady, probing thrust of his arousal turning her bones to liquid. Her mouth was still locked beneath the mind-blowing passion of his, her hands threading through the wet thickness of his hair, her legs no longer touching the bottom of the pool but curled around the hair-roughened length of his.

'I want you,' he growled against her mouth as he deftly untied the strings of her bikini top. 'Damn, it but I want you.'

Ava was vaguely aware of her top floating away as Marc's hands cupped her already peaking flesh. She gasped as his mouth covered hers again, her inner core beating with a pulse that was as strong as it was exigent. His tongue stroked and stabbed at hers simultaneously, making her breath catch with anticipation. Her heart raced with excitement, the sheer thrill of being in his arms again was beyond what she had imagined it would be. There was more heat, more urgency and more passion than ever before as kiss was exchanged for kiss, their teeth and tongues duelling until Ava had no idea who was in control any more.

Her hands left his hair and went to the cord of his bathers, untying it blindly as her mouth burned against his. She felt him spring into her hands as he stepped out of the bathers, the length of him heavy and hot with lust. She stroked him under the water, the rhythmic action as natural to her as breathing in spite of the five long years that had passed. She knew what he liked, how hard, how soft, how fast and how far she could go until he would check her movements before he lost control. She loved the feel of him; he was so strong and yet so vulnerable like this.

When he untied the strings of her bikini at her hips Ava drew in another little hitching breath of excitement. There would be no going back now. She could feel it in his body as it thrummed with need against hers. They had never made love in the water before. It was such a sensuous experience, the hint of the forbidden about it only adding to the allure.

She opened to him like a flower, gasping as he drove into her so thickly her back grazed the tiles of the pool. Her body clamped around him, waves of pleasure tingling through her with each deep thrust he gave. There was something so primal about his lovemaking; the pounding urgency of it made it her pulse soar. He was rough and fast, but she was with him all the way. Her body was humming with sensation as he drove harder and harder. She felt that delicious tight little ache start low and deep, the tight pearl of tension that needed just that little bit more friction for release to come.

She wriggled against him instinctively, wantonly, recklessly as she felt herself reach the summit of human sensation. She bit down on his shoulder to block her gasping cries of ecstasy, shuddering and convulsing as his body continued to pump within hers.

As she floated down from the heights of pleasure she heard him suck in a harsh breath before he gave a series of hard grunts as he spilled into her, his body tight as whipcord, his muscles clenched beneath her clinging fingers.

She felt him sag against her momentarily before he stepped back from her, raking a hand through his wet hair, his dark eyes briefly meeting hers before looking away.

'I'm sorry,' he said. 'That was not meant to happen, or at least not without protection.'

Ava gathered her pride, no easy feat when both pieces of her bikini were floating at the other end of the pool like an ill-formed octopus. How had she let herself be used by him? Where was her self-control? He had proved what her place in his life was going to be: as a sexual plaything he could access whenever he felt like it and she had given him every reason now to think she was more than willing to participate. She hadn't even had the presence of mind to insist he use protection. Didn't that prove how wanton he thought her to be? 'Wasn't it your intention to show me my place?' she asked with a flinty glare.

The space between his dark brows narrowed. 'Ava, this was always going to happen,' he said, brushing his wet hair back again, his chest still rising and falling as his breathing slowly returned to normal. 'Maybe it would have been wiser to have done it indoors and with less haste, but that's not something that can be changed. I will make it up to you right now. Let's go inside and I'll show you.'

She threw him a withering look before turning and climbing out of the pool. 'No, thank you,' she said, snatching up her towel off the deck and wrapping it around herself tightly.

Marc vaulted out of the water and stopped her with a hand on her arm. 'Wait, Ava,' he said crossly, although he was annoyed with himself more than her. He had caught sight of a graze on her back, a reddened patch that made him feel ashamed of himself for losing control. 'Let me see your back. It looks like it's sore.'

She tried to slap his hand away. 'Get away from me. It's obvious what I'm here for—your pleasure, in any way and any place and any time you like it. Douglas might have had his faults, but he never once made me feel the way you have just done.'

Marc felt each of her words hit him like lethally aimed arrows, but he kept his expression mask-like. 'You felt pleasure too, Ava, or are you going to deny it just to spite me, hmm?'

She threw him an icy glare. 'Think what you like. I might have been pretending for all you know.'

Marc chuckled at her spirited defiance. 'Then that was a pretty amazing performance, Ava.' He rubbed a hand over the indentation her teeth had made on his shoulder. 'But I know your body and I know an orgasm when I feel it, both yours and mine.'

Her eyes glittered with hatred, her body almost vibrating with the effort of containing her anger, but he wondered if she was furious with him or with herself for responding to him so unrestrainedly. Perhaps she had wanted to insult his pride by withholding her pleasure, but it had been such a powerfully explosive moment it had taken her by surprise, just as it had him. God knew, his body was still humming with the aftershocks of having her in his arms again. He couldn't wait to repeat the experience, time and time again.

But there were questions that required some answers first.

He reached for his towel on the sun lounger where he had left it earlier, and tied it roughly around his hips. 'You never did give me a straight answer to my question. Why did you give your sister the bulk of the money Cole gave you?'

She elevated her chin in a haughty manner. 'That is between Serena and me.'

Marc tightened his jaw as he held her fiery gaze. 'Has she got some sort of drug or gambling problem?'

She glared at him for suggesting such a thing. 'That is exactly the sort of thing you would think, isn't it, Marc?' she said. 'Think the worst before any other possibility comes to mind.'

'If there is nothing to hide then why not tell me what she has needed your financial help for?' he asked, fighting down his frustration. She was so wilful and defensive he couldn't get a straight answer out of her. He hated not knowing all the facts. It made him feel as if she had the power to tug the rug from under his feet. He was certainly not going to allow her the chance to do that again. Not in this lifetime.

She held his gaze for several taut seconds before lowering hers, a whoosh of a sigh passing through her soft lips. 'Serena can't have children,' she said, 'or at least not naturally. I've been helping her and Richard pay for repeated IVF treatments.'

Marc absorbed the information for a moment. He wondered why Ava had been so determined to keep such a thing quiet. It was a wonderful gesture on her part and, given how she had been painted in the Press, he couldn't understand why she hadn't used her acts of goodwill to whitewash her reputation. Surely it would have gone a long way to turn the public's opinion around. But then her sister's privacy probably had a lot to do with it, if not Serena's husband, he thought. Marc had only met him once and only briefly at that, but Richard Holt had struck him as a rather conservative English gentleman who would no doubt be appalled at having such sensitive private issues hung out in public.

'Thank you for telling me,' he said. 'It will go no further than me if that is what you wish.'

Her grey-blue eyes came back to his, a shadow clouding them. 'My sister has suffered a lot over the years,' she said. 'Not just with the fertility issue, but long before that. Losing our mother was hard for both of us, but I think Serena, being that bit younger, felt it more, especially when our father remarried so quickly. I tried to protect her as much as I could but I didn't always succeed.'

Marc frowned as he took it all in. Ava seemed to be blaming herself for not doing a job she was far too young to be doing at that time. No one could replace someone's mother. He should know—the loss of his had deeply affected him, even though the circumstances were totally different. It made him wonder how far Ava would go to protect her sister, if in fact her marriage to Cole had been for exactly that purpose and no other. It was an uncomfortable thought that Marc himself had acted no less ruthlessly by forcing her into a loveless union for his own ends. Ava had sacrificed herself all over again in order to bring about her sister's happiness. Marc had always known Douglas Cole was a shady character who thought nothing of the odd dodgy deal, but what he couldn't stomach or even bear to think about was how Ava had been used as a pawn and he had added to her suffering by insisting on her becoming his mistress again. He was so used to looking upon her as the guilty one: the betrayer, the harlot who had stomped all over his pride by leaving him for another man, he hadn't stopped to think what other motive she might have for acting as she had. No wonder she hated him with such vehemence. She might have capitulated to primal desire as he had done, but it didn't mean she cared anything for him. Why would she? He had judged her without mercy, blackmailed

her and virtually stripped her of her freedom
for the sake of his pride. How he would ever
make it up to her was beyond him at that
point. He needed time to think. He was not
used to being flooded by such a tidal wave
of emotion, guilt being the primary one. It
made him feel defensive, as if he needed to
build a wall around himself until he could
navigate his way through the mess he had
made, to make some sense of where to go to
from here.

He watched in silence as Ava gnawed at
her lip and continued, 'I just want Serena to
be happy. She had a terrible experience when
she was a teenager. On her very first date she
was sexually assaulted. It took years for her
to get over it. I was worried she was going
to…to…end it all, but thankfully I finally
managed to get her the help she needed.
Throughout the whole time, our father was
next to useless and our stepmother even
worse. They thought she was making it up to
get attention.'

Marc felt a gnarled hand clutch at his
insides. 'You are indeed a very devoted sister,'
he said. 'I hadn't realised how much you had
done for her over the years. I am sorry.'

She gave him a fleeting look before

turning away. 'Serena wants a baby more than anything. She's finally found a man who absolutely adores her. Richard is so gentle and loving, so perfect for her. He would love her with or without having a family, but she is so very determined to give him a child.'

'I would imagine it would be a big thing for a woman,' Marc said. 'It's the sort of thing one takes for granted—fertility, I mean.'

She ran her tongue over her lips and glanced at him again before shifting her gaze. 'Yes…yes, I suppose it is…'

There was a three-beat silence.

'I know I asked you before, but in the light of what happened in the pool a few minutes ago…' Marc cleared his throat as he pushed back his hair with his fingers 'you *are* currently taking the Pill, are you not? If you weren't sleeping with Cole then you wouldn't need to be on it, unless, of course, you had other lovers.'

Her face coloured, but Marc wasn't sure if it was anger at being reminded of the reckless passion they had just shared, or whether she was embarrassed at discussing such personal issues. She had not exactly been prudish with him in the past, so he could only assume she was still furious with him for demonstrating she could still respond to him in spite of all her words to the contrary. He had to admit he was a little annoyed with himself for not holding back a little longer. It gave her power over him, the sort of power he didn't want her to have, to know she still had such an overwhelming effect on him. Given how he had treated her, what would stop her from using it against him? She could go to the Press and destroy him in a few choice paragraphs. Would she do it? Could he afford to trust her? Surely she had even more reason now to try and destroy him.

Marc set his mouth. 'I understand you are angry at me and I don't blame you. I have got a lot of things wrong, some by my own arrogance, but also from you keeping secrets that had no need to be kept. But while you may not have had a sexual relationship with Cole, how am I to know if you have had other lovers unless you tell me?'

'You have nothing to worry about as far as I am concerned,' she said in a self-righteous manner, pulling her towel tighter around her body. 'I have not been sleeping around, but then you might choose not to believe me, of course.'

Marc knew he deserved that little swipe of hers, but he could not have rested until he'd asked. It was going to take him some time to process all she had told him. She had said nothing of her sister's situation in the past, but then he hadn't told her half of his own background. Their relationship back then had been based on lust and very little else, or at least from his perspective. He knew Ava had wanted more from him, but he had sworn off marriage after seeing what happened to his father. It had been gut-wrenching to see a fully grown man totally shattered by the desertion of his wife. Marc had vowed from a young age he would never allow his heart to be engaged in any of his relationships with women. And he had been true to that vow. He had always kept things light and casual, or at least until Ava had come along. She was the first woman he had not been able to forget. It maddened and frustrated him that he had not been able to move on. If he had acted like a sensible adult none of this would have happened. He should have accepted her decision to end their relationship. The trouble was he had wanted her so much. He *still* wanted her. He wondered if there would ever be a time when he didn't.

'I will use condoms in future, just to be sure there are no accidents,' he said with perhaps a little less finesse than was called for. 'I don't want any nasty surprises.'

Ava stiffened in anger. 'You think I would do something like that?'

He bent down to scoop his bathers out of the pool, wringing them out in his hands and then stepping into them with no hint of self-consciousness. 'It has happened before,' he said. 'I know of several men who've suddenly had their lives turned upside down by a paternity case thrown at them by an ex-lover.'

Ava clutched at the knot of her towel. 'This is a totally hypothetical question, but if—and it's a big and very unlikely if—*if* I was to fall pregnant, what would you expect me to do?'

He finished retying the cord of his bathers before he answered. 'First of all I would expect to be told about it as soon as possible.'

'Why?' Ava shot back. 'So you could make the decision for me?'

'Don't put words in my mouth, Ava,' he said, frowning down at her. 'I merely said I would like to know as soon as it is humanly possible. As to what you decide…well, I have always believed it is a woman's choice, since ultimately it is her body that is involved.'

Ava met his gaze, her chin at a combative height. 'I wouldn't dream of having an abortion. I think you need to know that right from the start.'

'I would not ask it of you,' he returned. 'Especially given the trouble your sister is experiencing.'

Ava was surprised by the empathy in his voice as he spoke of her sister. She bit her lip and sank down to sit on the end of the sun lounger behind her. 'At least Serena has Richard by her side,' she said to fill the stretching silence.

'How many IVF attempts have they made?' Marc asked.

She shrugged. 'I've kind of lost count… six…maybe seven.' She looked at her hands resting on her thighs. 'The last miscarriage…the one she's just had has been the worst for her. Everything was going so well and then…' She bit down on her lip again, her eyes misting over.

Marc put a hand on her shoulder, his palm tingling at the contact with her soft, silky skin. 'It is not your fault your sister cannot have children. It seems to me you are going out of your way to see that she gets every chance to have a family.'

She looked up at him. 'Why have you always been so against having children?'

He dropped his hand from her shoulder and moved to the other side of the terrace, his gaze taking in the view without really seeing it. 'I have seen what happens when children are shunted back and forth between warring parents. I don't want to be responsible for that sort of emotional damage.'

After a lengthy silence he heard her rise from the sun lounger behind him. 'The sun is starting to burn me,' she said. 'Do you mind if I go inside and take a shower?'

Marc turned and looked at her. 'Ava, you don't have to ask my permission over every little thing.'

Her slim brows rose in twin arcs of cynicism. 'Don't I?'

He held her challenging gaze. 'You are not my slave, you are my current lover.'

'Is there a difference I should be made aware of?' she asked with that haughty look she had perfected that made Marc's hands itch to reach for her and kiss her senseless.

'What happened here a few minutes ago is not over,' he said. 'Rather it is just beginning. If you are not careful, *ma petite*, I will demonstrate it right here and now.'

She turned and stalked across the terrace and back into the villa, leaving Marc with nothing but the afternoon breeze to tease him with her lingering fragrance.

CHAPTER FIVE

Ava was surprised when she came downstairs for dinner to find Celeste had set the large formal dining table for only one. 'Is—er—Signor Castellano not here for dinner this evening?' she asked the housekeeper.

Celeste smoothed a tiny crease out of the starched white tablecloth. 'He said he had some business to attend to at his office,' she said.

'I didn't realise he had an office in Monte Carlo,' Ava said, frowning as she took her seat.

Celeste gave her an unreadable look. 'He does not yet have an office here, although I believe he is in the process of setting one up,' she said. 'He flew to London an hour ago.'

Ava tried not to show how much the news affected her, but even so she felt as if she had been kicked in the stomach. Marc's passionate attention this afternoon out at the pool had stirred her senses into a frenzy from which they had yet to recover. To hear from someone else he had left for London hurt far more than it ought to have. Was he deliberately showing her what he expected her position in his life to be? She was nothing more than a chattel, a plaything he picked up and put down whenever he felt like it. Business came first, as it had in the past. She was a part-time lover, a position she had sworn she would never be in again.

He couldn't have chosen a more effective tool to make her uncertain of him, to stop her from feeling even the tiniest bit secure in his life: making mad, passionate love with her one minute, leaving her to fend for herself the next.

'Did Signor Castellano tell you when he is expecting to return?' Ava asked as Celeste brought in a tray with the first course.

'He said he would call you in a day or two,' Celeste answered. 'He left his contact details near the telephone in the library if you should need to reach him.'

Ava drummed her fingers on the table once the housekeeper had left. She was determined *not* to call him. She was going to carry on with her life as if he had not barged back into it, issuing his commands right, left and off-centre as if she had no will and mind of her own.

The following morning Ava left the villa, taking her time over browsing in the shops, stopping for a coffee and a pastry before making her way to a beauty spa, where she treated herself to a wash and blow-dry of her hair as well as a manicure and pedicure. She was on her way out of the spa when she ran into the wife of Douglas's business manager, a woman in her early thirties who dressed—and on far too many occasions acted—as if she were half that age.

'Ava!' Chantelle Watterson cooed as she air-kissed Ava's cheeks. 'You look absolutely marvellous. And no wonder, eh?'

'Er—well, I just had my hair and nails done, so—'

Chantelle threw back her bottle-blonde head and laughed. 'Droll, darling, very droll. I'm talking about your new lover. He is *gorgeous* and much younger than Dougie too, you lucky thing. I read about it in the paper. I am *so* envious, I just can't tell you. Hugh is starting to show his age, not just in appearance, if you know what I mean. Not that I mind really—I keep myself occupied.' She gave a meaningful wink.

Ava ground her teeth behind her forced smile. 'Hugh always looks wonderful for his age.'

'If it wasn't for his money I wouldn't stay with him, you know,' Chantelle said in a conspiratorial tone as she slipped a too thin, too tanned arm through one of Ava's. 'But then, beggars can't be losers, right?' She cackled at her own joke before continuing, 'I think it's time we had a drink to celebrate your new life.'

'Actually, I have to get going,' Ava said, trying to extract herself from Chantelle's python-like hold. 'Marc will be expecting me.'

Chantelle's green eyes glinted. 'Liar,' she said. 'He's in London right now with Hugh. It's something to do with the takeover of Dougie's company. Hugh was quite worried about it. But I suppose Marc doesn't talk to you about business, eh?'

Ava pressed her lips together. 'There's hardly been time to talk about anything,' she said.

'Yes, well, Hugh told me Marc Castellano moves quickly when he wants something,'

Chantelle said. 'But a word of advice, darling—men like Marc like things their way and their way only. If I were you I wouldn't make a fuss if he plays around behind your back or indeed right under your nose. I know for a fact Hugh's had a few flings, but what's the point in rocking the boat when it's sailing in the direction you want it to go?'

Ava couldn't wait to get away from the woman's gold-digging cynicism. She felt tainted by just being in her presence. 'Look, Chantelle, I really have to go,' she said, this time managing to get her arm out of the older woman's grip. 'Things are not what you think with Marc and me. We were together in the past. We are trying to make a go of it this time. I wouldn't want you or anyone to get the wrong impression or anything. You know how the Press has always had it in for me.'

Chantelle smiled a bleached-white smile that fell a little short of genuine. 'I understand perfectly, darling,' she purred. 'Marc Castellano is super-rich and super-sexy. You'd be a fool to let him slip through your fingers. Get a ring on your finger though and quickly. The Press can say what they like, but once you're legally his wife they'll leave you alone. That's what happened with me, in any case.'

'We have no intention of marrying at this point,' Ava said, even though for some reason it hurt to say it out loud.

Chantelle patted Ava's arm in a patronising manner. 'Then see if you can get him to change his mind,' she said, winking suggestively.

Ava made good her escape when another acquaintance of Chantelle's came out of the spa and diverted her attention.

As she made her way back to the villa Ava felt sick at the thought of being associated with someone as shallow and selfish as Chantelle Watterson. She had always hated the thought of people assuming she had hooked up with Douglas Cole for the very same reasons Chantelle had married Hugh Watterson. But for Serena's sake she had put up with it, being—back then—reasonably confident it wouldn't be long before she would move to the other side of the globe and put it all behind her.

Douglas had told her from the start about his diagnosis of bladder cancer; however, he had wanted no one else to know for the sake of his business. He had said he was worried about investors pulling out if they knew he was terminally ill. He had said he had been given less than two years to live, but he had made it to five. Ava often wondered if he had lied to her about his prognosis but she had no way of finding out now. Although the five years at times had felt like a prison sentence, she felt she had done the right thing in staying with him that final year so at least he was not left to die alone.

Another three days passed without any contact from Marc and Ava began to hover around the villa phone as well as keeping her mobile switched on and with her all the time. It annoyed her that he was able to keep her on such tenterhooks in spite of her determination to carry on as normal. The trouble was the villa seemed to have breathed in the very essence of him. Everywhere she went she felt his presence. Even swimming in the pool made her feel every sensation he had evoked in her, unsettling her to the point where she came in after only a couple of laps. She felt him on her skin, she felt him in her body, even her inner muscles tweaked with the memory of him possessing her. The red patch on her back had almost faded, but she still found her fingers going to it, tracing over it as she pictured Marc thrusting into her so roughly, as if he couldn't contain his need of her. Her breasts, too, ached for the cup of his hands or the suck of his mouth. Day after lonely day she had to distract herself from thinking about him, holding her emotions in check in case they flooded out of control.

After giving up on a swim, Ava showered and changed and came downstairs to her favourite sitting room, which overlooked the port of Monte Carlo. She stood at the windows with her arms folded across her middle, and sighed with a combination of boredom and frustration.

'Don't tell me you are missing me after only four days.' Marc's voice sounded from behind her.

Ava spun around so quickly she felt the room tilt. She put a hand to her throat where it felt as if her heart was going to beat its way out. 'When did you get back?' she asked in a breathless gasp.

He reached up to loosen his tie. 'Just then,' he said, his face cast in an expressionless mask. 'Celeste told me on her way out that you were in here.'

Ava fixed him with an arch look, the anger

she had felt at how he had left her dangling quickly replacing her shock at his sudden appearance. 'So how was your trip to London?' she asked. 'Was it business or pleasure or did you manage to squeeze in a bit of both?'

He closed the distance between them, stopping just in front of her, not touching her but close enough for her to feel his body heat. 'As my paid mistress, do you think you have got the right to question my movements when I am not with you?' he asked coolly and calmly.

Ava felt the anger swell in her veins until she thought she would explode with it. She raised her chin at him defiantly, her eyes throwing live wires of hatred at him. 'If I am to remain faithful to you I want you to do the same for me. In fact, I insist on it.'

'You sound rather adamant about it,' he said with that same mask-like expression. 'Has my absence made you feel unsure of your position in my life, *cara*?'

Ava was not going to admit to it even though it was painfully true. 'I am not going to share my body with you unless I am absolutely sure I am your only lover,' she said through lips pulled tight with determination.

He captured her chin, holding her gaze to his. 'You want exclusivity?'

'Yes. I won't settle for anything else.'

His eyes devoured hers as the silence beat like a tribal drum between them. Ava felt every one of her heartbeats; they seemed to be following a hectic syncopated rhythm instead of their usual slow and steady pace. Her breathing too was ragged and uneven, her lungs tight with the pressure of containing her spiralling emotions. She couldn't help dipping her gaze to his mouth, wondering if he was going to kiss her. If he did she would be lost. She could feel the pulse of need beating deep inside her. She had felt it the whole time he had been away and now he was here, touching her, she felt as if she would die without the pressure of his lips on hers.

'All right, but I have a few conditions of my own,' Marc said. 'I forbid you to be seen with or speak to or make any contact whatsoever with Chantelle Watterson. Do I make myself clear?'

Ava frowned at the implacability of his tone. 'She is not a close associate of mine. I hardly know her.'

'You were seen talking to her for half an hour the day after I left.'

Her mouth dropped open. 'You really are having me watched, aren't you? My God, but you've got some nerve, Marc. I have a right to my privacy.'

He released her chin and stepped away to shrug himself out of his jacket, hanging it over the back of the chesterfield before facing her again. 'There are some things I am prepared to negotiate on in our relationship, but gossiping with that gold-digging cow of a woman Hugh Watterson was fool enough to marry is the very last thing I will allow.'

'I don't gossip and I only met her by chance,' Ava insisted. 'I had my hair done and ran into her as I came out of the salon.'

'That is not the way she told it to Hugh,' he said.

'So you'd rather believe what she said to him than what I am saying to you?' she asked bitterly.

His expression remained shuttered. 'I am just asking you to keep away from her, that is all. I don't want the Press to get the wrong idea about your association with her. I know you won't believe it, but I am trying to protect you.'

Ava rolled her eyes. 'You're right, I don't believe you. I thought the whole idea of this arrangement of yours was to cause as much damage to my reputation as you could.'

His brow darkened with a frown. 'Look, Ava, I'm still working through some issues. It's become more and more apparent to me that I have not always acted with the sort of propriety I should have, given the circumstances. It's taking me some time to see things from your perspective.'

'Take all the time you want,' she said with a scornful toss of her head. 'But given your cynical take on life, I reckon it will take a decade or two before you begin to trust any woman, let alone me.'

'I wasn't planning on continuing our affair quite that long.'

Ava felt as if he had just backhanded her. Her whole body stung with the aftershock of his clinically delivered statement, pain reverberating until she felt as if she was going to pass out.

'Is something wrong?' Marc asked, reaching for her as she swayed in front of him. 'You've gone completely white.'

'I—I'm fine…' She brushed off his hand, her eyes falling away from his. 'I haven't had much to eat today. It's been too hot.'

'Celeste told me you haven't been eating properly for some weeks now,' he said, still frowning as he took in her pallid features. 'Do you think you should see a doctor?'

'No. I'm just not quite over a stomach bug I picked up when I visited my sister a couple of weeks ago.'

Marc waited a moment before he asked, 'Are you missing him?'

She looked at him blankly. 'Missing whom?'

Marc had brooded over it the whole time he was away, wondering if, in spite of her platonic relationship with Cole, deep down she had come to love him. After all, she had lived with him for five long years and nursed him through to his death. All the people he had spoken to in the London branch of Cole's business had confirmed how much Ava had done for him. How committed she had been to seeing that every one of his needs was met no matter what the time of day. Marc had gone away in order to gain perspective, to regroup and yet he had ended up even more confused about her motives. Ava McGuire had married a dying man—a very rich, old dying man. What better odds for her than that? She might not have slept with Cole, but that didn't mean she wasn't a gold-digger. She had banked on a big payout at the end, but now Marc was standing in the way of it. 'Your husband,' he said, jealousy rising like bile as he said those most hated of words.

Her throat rose and fell, the colour flowing back into her face as if someone had turned on a tap inside her. 'I would be a very cold person indeed if I could live with someone for five years and not miss them when they were gone,' she said. 'He deserves to be grieved. I know he was ruthless in business and he didn't always do the right thing by his family, but at least he tried to fix things before he died.'

Marc hated hearing her praise the man who had stolen so much from him. He hated thinking about the long hours he'd had to work to rebuild his business after Cole had won the bid over his. He had always believed Ava had been an active part of that betrayal, but based on the evidence he had gathered over the last few days it seemed more and more likely that Cole had worked alone. How much Ava knew of how she had been used was still open to investigation. There were still piles of papers to go through, but Marc was determined to uncover every motivation, both Cole's and Ava's. He had worked so hard for so long on exacting his revenge, he had hated Ava for five years; every thought he'd had was about having her back where he wanted her. The irony was he had her exactly where he had worked to get her, but she still wasn't his. He could see it in the way she looked at him. Hatred glittered in her grey-blue gaze, almost stinging him with its cold, hard intensity. She had used to look at him with such open adoration. He had found it claustrophobic at the time, but now he felt as if he would give anything to see her eyes soften and glisten with anything but the loathing he saw there now.

'Hugh Watterson told me how devoted Cole was to you,' Marc said. 'And yet you deny having been in love with him.'

Her eyes met his briefly before moving away again. 'There are many types of love,' she said. 'The love one feels for a parent, for instance, is quite different from that one feels for a friend or a lover.'

'So the love you felt for him was more parental than anything else?'

She gave him an irritated look. 'Could we please talk about something else?' she asked. 'Like why you felt you could just fly off to London without telling me when you were leaving or how long you would be away?'

'I had an issue to see to that cropped up without notice,' he said. 'I had to catch the first available flight. There wasn't even time to pack a bag, let alone discuss my plans with you. I told Celeste on my way out to inform you of my absence.'

'I suppose you think it's amusing to make me look like a fool in front of the staff,' she tossed back crossly.

'It seems to me you have the full support of the staff,' Marc returned, 'Celeste in particular.'

'Celeste has been at this villa a long time,' she said. 'She was extremely fond of Douglas, for all of his faults. She of all people knows how much I did for him.'

Marc felt his insides twist all over again with jealousy. 'Yes, I have been hearing the same thing time and time again from Cole's London staff. It seemed you made quite an impression on everyone you met as the devoted, loving, self-sacrificing little wife, right to the very end.'

Her eyes threw flick-knives of disdain at him. 'Self-sacrifice is not something you are familiar with, is it, Marc? You have always put your interests first and, from what I've seen so far, nothing has changed.'

He blocked her with his arm as she made

to leave. 'No, I have not finished talking to you,' he said.

Ava tightened her mouth and then, still holding his gaze, dug her fingernails into the flesh of his arm.

He swore and pulled his arm away, reaching for his handkerchief to dab where her nails had almost broken the skin. 'You have developed claws, *ma petite*,' he said calmly as he briefly touched her lips with his finger.

Ava felt her spine loosen at the gentleness of his touch. She felt herself drowning in the dark depths of his coal-black gaze, the silence growing, swelling, burgeoning with the erotic tension that buzzed like electricity between them. Her body responded to his closeness, her breasts feeling full and heavy, her belly quivering with flickers of longing, her inner core moistening at the promise of fulfilment she could see in his gaze just before it went to her mouth.

'Do not fight me, Ava,' he commanded softly, his breath feathering over the surface of her lips. 'Why not kiss me instead, hmm?'

Ava felt her eyelashes go down as her heels lifted off the floor to bring her mouth within touching distance of his. She pressed her lips softly to his, barely touching, breathing in his scent, his maleness, the heat and exhilarating potency of him.

He kissed her back equally softly, hardly any pressure, just a light, teasing touchdown of male lips on female, generating heat that was so combustible Ava could feel it like flames licking at her from deep inside her body.

His mouth slowly increased its pressure, his tongue stroking for entry, which she gave on a gasping sigh of pleasure. Her tongue caressed his, dancing with it, duelling with it until she finally allowed him to be the victor.

His hands cupped her face as he deepened the kiss, then his fingers were splayed in her hair, massaging, caressing her as his mouth worked its intoxicating magic on hers.

Ava pressed closer, wanting to feel the blood-thickened length of him where she needed him most. Her body felt so intensely alive, every part of her aching with need, fully charged to respond to him and him alone.

His mouth moved from hers down the side of her neck, searing kisses that burned her skin, his tongue a sexy rasp as it tasted each of her pleasure points. She threw her head back, delighting in the way he was taking his time, drawing out the pleasure to the point of torture.

By the time he got to her breasts she was close to begging. She whimpered breathlessly as he removed her clothing, piece by piece, in a reverse striptease that had her heart racing with excitement as each article hit the floor.

He was still fully clothed, which added to the daring sensuality of it. Ava reached for the zip on his trousers, but he pushed her hand away. 'Not yet, *cara*,' he said huskily. 'This is my chance to show you I have not forgotten how to take my time in pleasuring you.'

Ava shivered as he pressed her back against the leather-covered desk, her body splayed like a feast for him to devour. She was beyond shame; her need was too intense, far too out of control for her to think about how she might view this incredibly intimate act in the morning. Right now she wanted him to pleasure her; every nerve-ending was screaming for it, every cell of her body vibrating uncontrollably with the need for release.

She gasped as he stroked her first with his fingers, the slow-moving action arching her spine where it lay pressed against the desk.

She felt her own moisture, the slickness of it making every glide of his fingers that much more thrilling and erotic.

'You are so beautiful,' he said in a deep, gravelly tone. 'Like an exotic hot-house flower opening to the sun.'

Ava felt her sensitive nerves twitching in response to the waft of his warm breath as he brought his mouth to her. She drew in a sharp breath, holding it in her chest as he explored her with his tongue. The heart of her need gathered at that one pearl-like point; she felt the exquisite build-up, the growing wave-like tension taking over her completely. She couldn't think or feel anything other than what he was doing to her, the sensations he was evoking finally taking over. She felt herself shatter into a million pieces, each one a burst of bright, flashing colour, like fireworks exploding in a clear night sky. Her body rocked with the aftershocks, she was even vaguely aware of the ink well on the desk rattling as she convulsed with pleasure.

Almost as soon as the pleasure flowed out of her, the shame rolled in, great, giant waves of it, each one threatening to drown her. Ava propped herself up on her hands before sliding off the desk, bending to gather her clothes from the floor. She couldn't believe she had been so wanton again, let alone so foolish. By responding to him so feverishly she felt it had cheapened her, making her seem just like the pleasure-seeking gold-digger he thought her to be. She had acted like a sex-starved alley cat, opening her legs without hesitation every time he touched her. Did he have such power over her that she could act so recklessly with no thought to how it would make her feel or how he would look upon her?

'What are you doing?' Marc asked.

'What do you think I am doing?' she said, tugging at her bra, which was currently caught beneath his foot.

He bent down and picked it up for her. 'You seem in rather a hurry to leave.'

'The party is over, isn't it?' she asked, scrunching the bra into an odd-shaped ball. 'Or am I expected to service you?'

He frowned. 'Ava, there is no need for this petulance.'

She brushed her awry hair away from her face as she looked up at him. 'Aren't you going to make things a thousand times worse now by asking me whether I've done this, if not with Douglas, then with someone else?'

His jaw worked for a moment as if his mind was filling with the images of her writhing on the desk under someone else's caresses. 'No, actually I was not going to ask you that,' he said in a clipped tone. 'I know for a fact you did not sleep with Cole. That was another thing I found out from the ever-obliging Celeste. Cole was impotent and had been for many years as the result of surgery for his cancer.'

Ava pressed her lips together as she looked around for her shoes, privately marvelling at how Marc had managed to eke out so much information in so short a time from one of Douglas's most discreet and loyal staff members. It made her feel uneasy to think he had access to such intimate details. What if he found out the real reason behind her marriage to Douglas? As far as she knew Celeste knew nothing about it, unless Douglas had told her in the last stages of his illness as a deathbed confession. If Marc found out, how could she trust him not to expose Serena? What if he used Serena to get back at her?

'Answer me something,' Marc said. 'Did you know he was impotent when he asked you to marry him?'

Ava was still only partially dressed and a little too close to tears for her liking. 'I fail to see why that should be of any interest to you,' she said as she hunted about for her shoes. 'For God's sake,' she muttered in frustration. 'Where are my shoes?'

'They are over here,' he said, handing them to her. 'Answer the question, Ava. Did you know the full extent of Cole's condition when he asked you to be his wife?'

Ava clutched her pile of clothing close to her chest. 'He told me he was dying,' she said, not quite meeting his gaze. 'He told me he had two years at the most to live.'

'You must have been a much better wife than he bargained for,' Marc remarked wryly. 'You kept him alive for an extra three years.'

She gave him a cutting look. 'Are you finished with me now, Marc, or have you something else you require me to do as your paid mistress? I can get down on my knees if you like and return the favour, or would you rather a quick rough tumble on the floor?'

His eyes warred with hers for a stretching moment. 'I don't understand why you are being so testy about this deal between us, which as far as I can see is really no different from the deal you had with Cole, apart from a piece of paper, of course.'

Bitter tears burned at the backs of Ava's eyes, but she refused to allow them purchase. 'Everything is different about this deal between us,' she said. 'You have no idea how different.'

'Such as?'

'You hate me.' She said it like a challenge, willing him to deny it. When he said nothing in response Ava felt again as if he had slapped her.

One of her shoes thudded to the floor from the haphazardly gathered pile in her arms, but before she could retrieve it he bent down and picked it up and silently handed it back to her. 'Thank you,' she said tightly.

'If it is the amount I am paying you then all you have to do is say so,' Marc said after another taut silence.

Ava glared at him, knowing that if she didn't leave soon she would be howling like a child. 'It has *nothing* to do with the money.'

His brows lifted cynically. 'I beg to differ, *ma petite*, but it has everything to do with money,' he said. 'Are you forgetting the debts Cole left behind? That is why I had to go to London in such a rush. Hugh Watterson, your late husband's business manager-cum-accountant, has been skimming the books.'

Ava stared at him in open-mouthed shock. 'Are you sure Hugh is guilty? Have you any proof?'

The look in his eyes was like black stone. 'Of course I have proof. I have set my legal team to work to uncover every other discrepancy. I am sure I will find hundreds. Hugh is a very clever accountant. Over the last few months he has been busily stashing money in accounts where it was almost impossible to trace them.' He tipped up her chin, making her lock gazes with him. 'Was it a scheme you cooked up between you?'

Ava frowned until her forehead ached. 'What are you talking about? What scheme with whom?'

He kept his steely gaze on hers. 'You and Chantelle Watterson,' he said. 'When cornered Hugh said he did it for his young wife, to keep her in the manner to which she had become accustomed. You and she are very similar, are you not? You both hooked up with much older men, living a life of luxury in the hope that one day they would die and leave you their fortune. What a pity there was nothing left in the kitty for you when Cole conveniently obliged by dying while you were still young and attractive enough to start again.'

'That is a disgusting thing to say,' Ava said, stepping back in affront. 'I never wanted anything from Douglas.' *At least not for myself*, she thought.

'Now, that is not quite true, is it, Ava?' he asked. 'You would never have married him if he hadn't been filthy rich and terminally ill, now, would you?'

She raised her chin, meeting his gaze with fire in her own. 'He gave me an offer I felt compelled to accept. Anyway, it was more than you were ever going to offer me.'

The edges of his mouth flickered, as if anger was just beneath the surface, waiting to leap out and strike. 'I was always totally honest about what I was prepared to give you. I told you marriage was not an option for me.'

Ava continued to glare at him. 'It's not in your nature to compromise, is it, Marc? You just expect people to fall into your plans. Now, may I be excused, or do you want more bang for your buck?'

Marc unlocked his clenched hands, fighting every instinct to drag her into his arms and make love to her, to claim her in every way possible. His blood was thundering with the need to do so. But instead he gave a curt nod and stepped out of her way. 'I will see you in about a week's time,' he said. 'I have to fly to Zurich in the morning.'

He watched as she ran the point of her tongue out over her lips, a gesture of uncertainty or relief, he couldn't quite make up his mind which.

'I see,' she said. After a little pause she added, 'I take it you don't want me to come with you?'

He gave her an ironic look. 'Would you say yes if I asked you?'

The defiant glitter was back in her eyes like the flash of a silver sword. 'No, I would not.'

Marc smiled at her feistiness. He had plenty of time to tame her and tame her he would. 'Believe me, *cara*, if I wanted you with me you would not dare to say no,' he said, and before she could respond he strode out of the room, snipping the door shut behind him.

CHAPTER SIX

AVA was intensely annoyed that during the week while Marc was in Switzerland he did not once call her. But then, he didn't need to speak to her to know what she was up to, she realised after the very day he left, for as soon as she prepared to leave the villa a man dressed in a chauffer's uniform, standing beside a luxury car, greeted her on the gravel driveway, informing her he was at her service during Signor Castellano's absence.

'But I have no need of a driver,' Ava insisted. 'I always walk whenever I can and I'm only going to the gym at the health club.'

The man, who had introduced himself as Carlos, was equally insistent, holding the door open for her with an intransigent set to his features. 'It is not worth losing my job, Miss McGuire,' he said. 'I have a wife and a young family to support.'

Ava frowned in irritation. 'I am sure Signor Castellano would not be so heartless as to fire you just because I chose to use my legs instead of your services.'

'I have been given strict instructions to escort you wherever you need to go,' Carlos said. 'I am to keep you protected from the Press. Signor Castellano does not want you to be annoyed by the intrusion of anyone without him being there to protect you.'

She rolled her eyes as she got in the car. 'This is utterly ridiculous. I do not need a babysitter.'

'Think of me as a bodyguard, then,' Carlos said.

Ava scowled as she was driven to the health club, knowing full well Marc had only engaged the driver to tail her in case she took it upon herself to give an exclusive interview to the Press of what it was like being Marc Castellano's mistress. If she was indeed the type of woman like Chantelle Watterson, that was quite possibly what would occur. Ava, on the other hand, had no intention of speaking to anyone about her relationship to Marc.

She took a covert glance at the driver who seemed vaguely familiar. No doubt Carlos had been the spy Marc had had following her during his last absence. He didn't trust her. That was the problem that just wouldn't go away. Marc believed her to have betrayed him and no matter what she did or said to the contrary he was never going to believe or trust her word ever again.

But then, did *she* trust him? He had said—or at least intimated—he would abide by her rule of exclusivity while they were together, but how could she be sure he would hold true to it? He had a reputation as an international playboy, women chased him daily—she had seen enough pictures in the Press over the years to realise he was in no shortage of female company. He could just be paying lip service to her demands and she would have no way of knowing for sure if he was being unfaithful.

Jealousy ate at her with primitive teeth, the sharp incisors savage as they gnawed at her relentlessly when she thought of Marc flying from one country to another, enjoying his glamorous bits on the side while she waited here, trapped by his demands.

There were compensations, however; she had only that morning checked the balance in her bank account via the Internet and her eyes had rounded to the size of saucers at the amount Marc had deposited there. It gave her at least the comfort of knowing she could continue to support Serena in her quest to have a baby.

Almost unconsciously Ava laid one of her hands across the taut plane of her belly. A child with her was the very last thing Marc wanted and yet she felt a yearning so great to have a baby of her own it was almost painful to harbour the thought of never being able to create that incredible bond with him. She could imagine a little boy just like Marc with coal-black eyes and springy black hair with tiny dimples either side of his mouth when he smiled, which Marc so rarely did these days, or at least not without a hint of mockery to it, she thought with another painful pang. But there was no possibility of her becoming pregnant even though he had not used a condom when he had made love to her in the pool; she had been taking a low-dose Pill for years to control a tendency for painful periods.

After she had finished her routine at the health club Ava returned to the villa, not sure what else she could do. There were numerous books she wanted to read and myriad tasks she could help Celeste with, as had become her habit, but she felt restless and bored. She wanted a real job, not modelling, as she had done before, but one where she could use her brain instead of her body.

It was a long-held dream of hers to go back to the university degree she had deferred the year she had come to London to model for the UK branch of the agency she had modelled part-time for, and in order to accompany Serena on her gap year. Ava had been studying history and languages and had looked forward to one day being able to teach. Living in a place like Monte Carlo was a history-lover's dream. The principality had a long and colourful past, the royal dynasty that had held state for so long all part of the glamour and intrigue.

In the last year of their marriage Douglas had encouraged her to pursue her studies online, but just as she was about to enrol his condition had deteriorated. After his slow and agonising death, with all the things she'd had to see to since in packing up his things and sending them on to his family, she had not had the time to think too far into the future. And then, of course, there was the cost to consider. Studying didn't come for free, or at least not these days. She could end up like so many others with huge debts and no guarantee of a permanent job at the end of it.

And then there was Marc. Marc Castellano—the man she had once loved with all her being now hated her with a passion that was almost as great as his continued desire for her. He had a ruthless agenda to have her as his plaything, no strings, no love, just plain and simple sex at his command. Reducing their relationship to one of physical convenience for him was a form of emotional torment for her. She had no idea how long he would want her in his life; he had given her no clue, other than to state quite clearly it was not going to be for the long term.

The evening before Ava expected Marc to return to the villa she was sitting in her bedroom, reading a book on the Second World War, when there was a tap at the door. Assuming it was Celeste to come to say *bonsoir* before leaving for the day, she gave permission for entry.

The book almost fell to the floor when Marc stepped into the room. Her heart gave a galloping lurch as she gaze took in his tall, commanding presence. He was dressed in dark casual trousers and an open-necked white shirt which emphasised his olive skin and ink-black hair.

'You look surprised to see me, *cara*,' he said, closing the door with a tiny but, all the same, heart-stopping click.

Suddenly her room, which had always seemed so commodious in the past, shrank to the size of a doll's house. Ava felt as if the walls were pressing in on her, the air sucked right out of the space, making it almost impossible to pull in a much needed breath.

'I—I was not expecting you until tomorrow,' she stammered, putting the book to one side and standing up on legs that were not quite steady. She ran her damp palms down the front of her thin and years-old-cotton-pyjama-clad thighs, wondering if he noticed she had no make-up on, not even a smear of lip gloss. Her hair was tied back in a high pony-tail, still partially damp from her recent shower. She wasn't even wearing a bra beneath her faded pink tank top and her feet had ballet-flat-like slippers on instead of heels. It made her feel at a huge disadvantage without a veneer of sophistication to hide behind. Without her usual armour she felt like a schoolgirl of thirteen instead of a mature woman three years off turning thirty.

'I cancelled the last meeting,' he said. 'In any case, I had achieved what I had set out to achieve, so I caught the next available flight.'

Ava tucked a strand of hair that had escaped from her pony-tail behind one ear. 'I am sure you always achieve what you set out to achieve,' she said archly, trying to regain the ground she felt she had lost in being caught off guard by his unexpected arrival.

He came up close, so close she could smell the hint of citrus in his aftershave, the combination of lime and lemongrass and something else she couldn't quite identify, but it was no less captivating. She breathed it in, unconsciously holding her breath, physically and mentally preparing herself for his touch.

His dark eyes meshed with hers, studying her with an intensity that was both unnerving and exciting. She felt each of her heartbeats pounding in her chest, wondering if he knew how deeply unsettled she was by his proximity.

When his warm, dry palm cupped her left cheek, she felt her heart give another crazy lurch, her breath coming out on a jagged sigh.

'Did you miss me, *ma petite*?' he asked in a low, sexy tone.

Ava fought to control her response to his caressing, lover-like touch. 'Not at all,' she said crisply.

He smiled a knowing smile, his palm still cradling her face, his thumb now stroking against the curve of her cheek in a back and forth motion that was totally mesmerising. 'Celeste told me just before she left for the evening that you have been moping about with a downcast set to your features all week.'

Ava gave him a petulant look. 'If I gave her that impression it is only because you have me practically imprisoned here with your bodyguard on permanent watch. I can't take a step outside the villa without him insisting on driving me wherever I want to go, even if it is only within walking distance.'

He placed his hands on the tops of her shoulders. 'Why haven't you moved your things into my room?' he asked.

Ava was momentarily thrown off course by his rapid change of subject, a tactic she was starting to see he used to his advantage time and time again. 'I…I didn't realise you wanted me on call twenty-four hours a day,' she said, hoping he couldn't hear the betraying wobble in her voice.

His eyes were like a force field as they held hers and his hands tightened on her shoulders. 'I want you in my bed,' he said. 'I want to know that when I come home you will be waiting for me.'

'You are living in the wrong century, Marc,' she said with a flash of defiance. 'Slavery was abolished long ago.'

His mouth curled up at the corners, not quite a smile, but close enough to make Ava's heart skip a beat. 'Are you annoyed with me for not taking you with me to Zurich?' he asked.

She rolled her eyes in a scathing manner. 'Why should I be annoyed? I would be bored to tears sitting around in hotel rooms waiting for you to return.'

'Like you were here, *sì*?'

Ava marvelled at his perspicacity, but her expression—she hoped—gave nothing away. 'I am not used to being idle,' she said. 'I want to use my brain instead of filling in the day having my hair or nails done.' She took a little breath and announced, 'I want to go back to university and finish my degree.

I've already made some enquiries about doing a course online.'

The silence was so long she wondered if Marc could hear the sound of her heart beating. She could feel it inside her chest, hammering away like a jackhammer on performance-enhancing supplements.

'Are you informing me of your intentions or asking for my permission?' he finally asked.

She moistened her dry lips with a dart of her tongue. 'Do I need to ask your permission?' she asked, keeping her eyes locked on his.

His hands dropped from her shoulders. 'No,' he said, his expression like a mask. 'Of course not. I have no problem with you wanting to finish your degree. I think it's a great idea. It is impossible to overeducate yourself, *sì*?'

Ava looked up at him in astonishment. She had been so sure he would not agree to her plans she had been silently preparing herself for a showdown. Instead she felt strangely at sea, the wind suddenly too far away to inflate her self-righteous sails. 'Er—yes,' she said, running her tongue over her bare lips again. 'That's great, then. I can start straight away.

I've already been reading some of the recommended texts. I will get some credit for the subjects I've already completed, not much, but enough to...' She stopped rambling when she saw the bottomless wells of his eyes studying her silently.

Her shoulders suddenly felt cold without the warm cup of his palms, her cheek still tingling from his earlier caress. Her heart was beating too hard and too fast, her stomach doing complicated little gymnastic routines that made her feel disoriented.

The silence stretched and stretched and stretched, like a rubber band being pulled by an invisible hand. Ava felt as if at any moment the air was going to snap with the incremental build-up of tension she could feel vibrating in the space between them.

'You look like a schoolgirl with your hair tied up like that,' Marc said in a gruffly masculine tone.

Ava felt a blush steal into her cheeks, which she knew was only adding credence to his words. 'I was getting ready for bed...' She blushed even further and stumbled on gauchely, 'Um...I mean, I'd just had a shower and was about to turn in when you...you...took me by surprise...'

One of his hands reached behind her head and began toying with her pony-tail, the sensation of him coiling it around his fingers making her scalp quiver in delight. His hold was loose, playful almost, but she felt the underlying tension, the daunting but delicious possibility of him tugging her towards his mouth and hard, powerful body making her heart beat all the faster. Her gaze wandered over his face, finally coming to rest on his mouth. He was in need of a shave, his jaw was peppered all over with dark shadow that she knew from experience would rasp sexily against her softer skin.

'You know, Ava, lovers usually kiss when they greet each other after an absence,' Marc said, glancing at her soft mouth before returning to her grey-blue gaze.

'Are you informing me of your intentions or asking for my permission?' she asked, throwing his words back at him in a pert tone.

His fingers coiled her hair like a rope, bringing her inexorably closer. He felt her breath on his face, the fresh mint and womanly essence of her making his groin instantly swell with blood. He rubbed up against her, letting her know how she was affecting him, gauging her reaction.

She looked up at him with widening pupils, her soft lips slightly apart, and her breathing rate gradually increasing. Her breasts were jammed against his chest, the tight buds of her nipples detectable through the fabric of his shirt. The feel of her feminine mound so close to his erection was mind-blowing. He ached to feel her slick, tight body enclose him, to take all of him inside her, each and every one of her inner muscles rippling and clenching as he thrust into her.

He slowly released the tie that bound her hair, letting it fall in a fragrant cloud around her shoulders. Without saying a word he lifted the bottom of her tank top. She put her arms up, her breasts full and rosy-peaked as he lifted the top over her head and tossed it to one side.

Her eyes meshed with his, the want, the need, the expectation he could see reflected there so like what he was feeling it momentarily stopped him in his tracks. It had always been like this from the first time they had met. Her eyes had fascinated him, their smoky-grey and blue-flame depths had captivated him, luring him into a sensual orbit he had never been able to escape. He wore the memory of her body on his skin. It was like a perfume he couldn't wash away. No one else before or since had affected him as she did. Her femininity, the dainty softness and yet athletic strength of her excited him.

The air of mystery about her now made her all the more irresistible. There were secrets in the moving shadows of her eyes, things he had not seen before but was now determined to uncover.

Marc ran his hands down Ava's slim waist to settle on her hips, holding her against his pulsing heat. He realised with a twinge of regret this was not the time for an inquisition. He knew enough about her to know if he pushed too hard she would clam up; her defiant streak would come to the fore, leaving him with a host of doubts to torture him into the long hours of the night.

Ava felt a sudden shift in mood and looked up at Marc with a mixture of wariness and un-certainty. She self-consciously crossed her arms over her breasts. 'Is something…wrong?'

The faraway look fell away from his gaze like heavy velvet curtains dropping in one quick movement over a stage. 'Nothing is wrong, *ma petite*,' he said and released his hold. He reached into his trouser pocket and handed her a long, thin jeweller's box. 'I bought something for you while I was away.'

Ava looked at the designer's name inscribed on the box and felt her heart give a little flutter. She had looked in that particular jeweller's many times, but it was the sort of place where price stickers were never placed in the shop front windows. She had no idea how much Marc had spent, but, putting her modesty aside for a moment, she opened the box to find an exquisitely beautiful diamond pendant, so fine and so delicate she knew the price would have been in at least six figures. 'I…I don't know what to say…' she faltered. 'It's beautiful…'

'Here,' he said, taking the box from her. 'Let me put it on you.'

She turned around, her skin shivering in reaction as his fingers brushed against her neck to fasten the pendant's clasp. He placed his hands on her shoulders again and turned her back to face him. The diamond rested just above her naked breasts, making her ache to feel his touch.

'Perfect,' he said, his eyes dark and intense as they held hers. 'The glitter of the diamond reminds me of your eyes when you are angry.'

Ava bit down on her bottom lip as she covered her breasts with her folded arms again. 'I guess it would look better if I was wearing something more glamorous than my oldest pyjamas.'

'I think it would look better if you were wearing nothing at all,' he said and untying her arms from across her body, scooped her into his arms as if she were a quarter of her weight.

'Marc, put me down. I'm—'

'At least five kilograms lighter than you were when we were together in the past,' he said, cutting her off mid-sentence. 'You are obviously not eating enough for all the activity you do.'

'You don't know anything about the activity I do,' Ava said, scowling, as he carried her through to the master suite.

His dark eyes lasered hers as he set her down in front of him, her body still pressed up against the warm sexiness of his. 'No, you are right, *tesora mia*,' he said with an inscrutable look. 'I know very little about your activities. Perhaps when there is an appropriate time you can tell me all about them, *sì*?'

Ava shifted her gaze from the laser beam of his to her hands, lying flat against his broad chest. She could feel the beating of his heart under her right palm, the *thump thump thump* so steady compared to her erratically skipping one.

Marc tipped up her face, making her look at him. 'I've missed you, *ma belle*. I have got used to you snapping at me. Tragic, isn't it?'

'Then why didn't you call me so I could snap at you on the phone?' Ava asked, looking into the black depths of his eyes, feeling herself melting as his lips curved upwards in a half-smile.

'I like to see you when I speak to you,' he said, bending down to press a light, brief kiss to her lips. 'I also like to feel you tremble beneath my touch.'

She pressed her lips together, tasting him, tasting the promise of passion that was brewing like a storm approaching. She felt it in his body, the surge of his flesh against her reminding her of how suddenly things could get out of hand. A kiss was never just a kiss with Marc; it was a prelude to a sensual on-slaught that would leave her tingling for hours later. Her body was already preparing itself, the moisture of arousal hot and wet between her thighs, the persistent ache of her breasts for his touch and the heavy pulse of longing that made her feel hollow and empty inside.

He took her hands from his chest and, turning them over, kissed each open palm in turn, his eyes still holding hers. She shivered each time his tongue dabbed at the very centre of her palm, an erotic mimic of what was to come.

His hands released hers to undo the buttons of his shirt. Ava lifted her hands to explore his tanned chest as each part of it was revealed: the sculptured pectoral muscles, the tightly coiled ridges of his erectus abdominus, trailing her fingertips through the sprinkling of masculine hair that arrowed down to disappear beneath the waistband of his trousers.

'Touch me,' he commanded softly, urgently.

Ava's heart gave a sideways movement as she saw the naked need in his glinting eyes. She undid his waistband, rolling down his zip over the proud bulge of his manhood, her fingers impatient to feel him skin on skin.

He shrugged himself out of his shirt and, heeling off his shoes, stepped out of his trousers as they slid to the floor, leaving only his black underwear. Ava traced him through the tented fabric, teasing him, watching as he sucked in a breath to keep control. She became more daring, slowly peeling back the fabric, allowing him the freedom he craved, cupping him and then making a circle with her fingers, moving up and down his shaft in a rhythmic motion that she knew he would not be able to tolerate for long.

'*Mon Dio*, no more,' he groaned, dragging her hand away.

She lifted one of her fingers to her mouth, her eyes holding his, tasting him, watching as his throat moved up and down as he fought to contain himself. She loved seeing him like this, fighting the rampant flames of his desire for her while she slowly but surely burned in anticipation.

He snatched in another breath and reached for her pyjama bottoms, almost wrenching them down her legs in his impatience. 'You are the only woman on this planet who can do this to me, do you know that, *ma belle*?' he asked, nuzzling at the side of her neck where every nerve seemed to be calling out for his attention.

'How do you know that if you haven't been with every woman on the planet?' she asked, shivering as his tongue found the shell of her ear.

'Don't talk,' he said, sucking on her earlobe. 'I just want you to feel.'

Ava felt her spine slowly unhinge as he worked his way to her breasts, the moment when his mouth closed over her right nipple making her gasp out loud. He did the same to her other breast, sucking and circling her with his tongue until the flesh was achingly tight and pulsating with sensation.

He pushed her down on the bed, gently but in a primal alpha-male manner that made her skin tingle in delight. He opened the bedside drawer and took out a condom, ripping open the packet and applying it with a deftness she could only assume came from extensive practice, a thought that was as painful as it was unwelcome.

Marc looked at her questioningly, obviously picking up some nuance on her face she hadn't been able to disguise in time. 'As much as I would like to do this bareback, Ava, I don't want to have to deal with the consequences if an accident should occur.'

Ava felt her heart contract, as if it were suddenly jammed between two house bricks. 'It's quite all right,' she said, injecting her voice with just the right amount of nonchalance. 'I don't want any accidents either.'

His eyes stayed on hers a fraction longer than she was comfortable with. It felt as if he was peeling back her skin, looking at her innermost desires, one by one.

'Things are different now,' he said. 'You understand that, *si*?'

She nodded and reached for him again, stroking the sheathed length of him, watching as his face contorted with the effort of holding back his response.

He nudged her thighs apart, one of his legs going over one of hers in an erotic tangle of limbs that awakened every nerve in her body in feverish excitement. He plunged into her, so deeply she winced, her fingers digging into his flanks to anchor herself as the unexpected pain gradually subsided.

She felt him check himself, coming up on his elbows to look down at her, a frown narrowing the distance between his impossibly dark eyes. 'I should have used some lubricant,' he said. 'Did I hurt you?'

Ava felt it then, it took her completely by surprise, but then just about everything about Marc these days took her by surprise. She hadn't expected her love for him to survive how he had handled their break-up; she hadn't expected her love for him to survive his ruthless demands and conditions…she hadn't expected her love for him to come back with such intensity she could feel it fill the aching emptiness of her soul like water filling a dam after a flash flood.

'Ava?'

She gave herself a mental shake and gazed into his eyes. 'Make love to me, Marc,' she said, her voice barely above a whisper.

He hesitated, as if he was waiting for something.

She placed her hands around his neck and pulled his mouth down to just above hers. 'Please?' she said.

'It will be my pleasure,' he said huskily and covered her mouth with his.

CHAPTER SEVEN

His kiss was like fire against Ava's lips, his tongue a sword of flame that burned her with each stab and thrust. She met his demands with feverish ones of her own, nipping at him with her teeth, sucking on his lower lip, pulling and releasing, teasing him, daring him to let his passion off the leash. She felt him straining to keep control, the tension building in his body as he re-entered her, slowly this time, waiting for her to stretch to accommodate him, her own silky moisture easing each of his movements within her.

His rhythm gradually picked up its pace, gently at first, but as she kept pace he moved on with increasing intensity, the friction against her sensitive nerves making her quiver in response. She could feel the way her body assembled all its feeling into one tightly budded point, the release she so desperately craved just out of her reach. She whimpered against his mouth as it kissed hers with tantalising thoroughness. She arched her spine, pushing her hips up to meet the downward thrust of his, but it seemed he was going to make her wait a little longer.

'Marc…' Her voice was a breathless whisper of sound. 'Please…oh, please… don't make me wait any longer…'

He increased his pace, his breathing hard as she urged him on with her hands and fingers pressed into his buttocks. The rocking of their bodies thrilled her, the way they fitted together so neatly. His hair-roughened limbs were such an erotic contrast to the creamy smoothness of hers, the strength of his taut muscles as they bunched beneath her touch making her breath catch in her throat. The pressure inside her was building up to a crescendo. She could feel every deep thrust of his send ripples of delight throughout her body. Her breasts were almost flattened beneath the pressure of his chest but she loved the scratchy feel of his masculine hair against her softness. It reminded her of how she used to trail her fingertips through it in the past, circling each of his hard flat nipples, kissing her way down to the throbbing heat of him until he exploded with passion.

Ava shifted restively beneath him, needing him to bring her to the ultimate moment, but too shy to ask. She felt him smile against her mouth as he reached down between their bodies, finding the core of her with heart-stopping accuracy, his fingers working at her, stroking slowly, gradually building his pace and pressure until she was gasping out loud. She was so close, agonisingly so, but suspended, hanging, dangling over a precipice so high it was terrifying.

'Let go, *cara*,' Marc coaxed gently. 'Come for me.'

'I can't,' she cried, writhing beneath him, her head thrashing about in frustration.

He stilled her with the cup of his palm against her cheek. 'Hey, look at me,' he commanded softly. 'It's me, Marc. You know how to do this—we've done this many, many times before, *sì*? Why should this time be any different?'

She opened her eyes and looked at him, her teeth biting into her lower lip, before she mumbled as her gaze fell away, 'I know… but it's…it's different now…'

'How is it different?' he said, slowly

stroking her again. 'I have not forgotten a thing about your body. I don't think I ever will forget how you respond to me.'

She choked back a little gasp and he increased the pressure ever so slightly, watching as she rode the wave right to the top before finally free-falling. She cried out, a high, keening cry that sent shivers cascading down his spine. He felt her body spasm and convulse around him, sending him mad with the desire to let go, but he waited until her release had faded.

'There,' he said, smiling. 'I knew you could do it. You just needed to relax and to trust me.'

She looked at him in wonderment, her eyes still glazed with passion, her creamy chest a rosy hue, signalling how intense her release had been. She reached up and touched him on the face, her fingers a light caress that made Marc wonder if she had not experienced pleasure with anyone since him. Had she been celibate for five long years? Had no other lover touched her? It was a surreal feeling to think he had been the last person to bring her pleasure. That she had not sought it elsewhere, even whilst married to Cole, as so many women in her place would have done. It made him wonder all over again why she had agreed to such a marriage. If she was of such integrity why then had she been bought for a price like the gold-digging opportunist the Press had made her out to be? Was there something he *still* didn't know about her reasons for marrying Cole? He had searched and searched and yet he still felt as if a part of the puzzle was missing. It annoyed him, like a grass seed in his sock. He kept looking for it but no matter how much it pricked him he couldn't locate it.

'Marc?' Ava traced her fingers over the flattened line of his mouth. 'Is something wrong?'

He rolled away from her, lying on his back to stare blankly at the ceiling.

Ava felt her stomach cave in, wondering if she had disappointed him in some way. His erection had subsided and she knew it wasn't because he had come. She knew him well enough to know the signs and she had been waiting for them, waiting for that pressure-cooker-like tension, the way his body would go rigid before pumping his way through his release. She felt cheated, even though she'd had the best, most intense orgasm of her life.

She reached out and touched his chest, her palm flat against his sternum. 'Did I do something wrong?' she asked.

He turned his head sideways to look at her, his dark eyes fathomless. 'No,' he said after what seemed a lifetime. He turned his head back and stared at the ceiling again, releasing a long and raspy-sounding sigh. 'It's not you, it's me.'

Ava pulled in a breath that felt as if it had barbs attached. She felt so unsure of herself. In the past if something like this had happened she would have seen to matters with her lips and tongue or even her hand and he would have been back in business within seconds.

She moved her hand experimentally, but as if he sensed her intentions, one of his came over it and stilled it.

'No,' he said, releasing her hand as he got off the bed. 'I'm not in the mood right now. Sorry.'

Ava felt assailed by doubts and insecurities. He had never spurned any of her advances in the past. Was he already tiring of her? She shrank back on the bed, pulling at the sheet to cover her nakedness. She watched as he silently dressed, each of his movements mechanical, as if his mind was elsewhere.

After he had disposed of the condom he turned and looked at her, his expression as unreadable as a blank sheet of paper. 'Maybe it is best if we keep to separate bedrooms,' he said, 'for the time being at least.'

Ava swallowed thickly, her heart feeling as if he had kicked it aside with one of his strongly boned feet. She moistened her lips, feeling vulnerable and perilously close to tears. 'If that's what you want,' she managed to say without a tremor in her voice.

He ran his hands through the thick pelt of his hair, leaving deep, finger-size trails. His jaw was moving beneath his skin, as if he was silently rehearsing the words before he got them out.

Ava held her breath, waiting for the words she dreaded. He was finished with her. He had set out what he hoped to achieve. He had extracted his revenge, he had made her beg. Well, she had well and truly done that, she thought with a scalding wave of shame. He couldn't have timed it better. Just when she realised she still loved him and would stay with him on any terms he was going to end it.

It was finished.

Over.

Finito.

The end.

'At the time of your marriage, or at any time leading up to it, did you know Cole was bidding for the same contract as me?' he asked, pinning her with his hawk-like gaze.

Ava moistened her lips, her mouth so dry she had to do it twice before she could speak. 'I know you will find this hard to believe, but I didn't know he was making a bid on the Dubai thing. I knew very little about that arm of his business at that point. I don't think he wanted me to know. I know that sounds terribly naïve of me, but it's the truth. By the time I found out about it I had already accepted his offer and signed a contract. I had no choice but to stick with it. I had already used some of the money.'

His expression revealed nothing to show he either believed or disbelieved her. 'So you married him and moved to Monte Carlo and lived as his wife, allowing everyone to think—including your sister—you were his wife in every sense of the word.'

Ava lowered her gaze. 'Serena knew the truth…about why I married Douglas…'

The room seemed to take a breath and hold it in the silence.

'And what was the reason, or am I to play

twenty questions for the next hour or two?'
Marc asked.

She pulled the sheet a little tighter around
her body as she got off the bed and slowly
raised her eyes to his. 'Because…' Her
tongue darted out to sweep over her lips.
'Because I did it for her.'

Marc felt as it something had just slipped
into place, making him feel a heavy,
clunking sensation somewhere in the middle
of his chest. He stared at her for another
stretching silence, mentally shuffling
through possible scenarios, none of them
making him feel particularly comfortable.
'Why?' he asked, surprised at how hoarse he
sounded.

Ava felt under siege. His questioning tech-
nique would have put a professional interro-
gator to shame. She felt a river of
perspiration roll drop by drop between her
shoulder blades to pool at the base of her
spine, which was currently doing a very poor
job of keeping her legs upright and steady.
Forgive me, Serena, she silently pleaded. *I
had to tell him some time. How could I let
this continue indefinitely, especially when I
love him so?* The words were spinning
around her head, making her feel dazed. She

hoped he would keep it to himself. She had put her trust in him; maybe it was foolish to do so, but after making love with him she had felt so vulnerable, so desperate for him to understand and find it in himself to forgive her for the past.

'Answer the question, Ava,' he said.

Ava slowly raised her chin, even though her insides were quaking. 'She'd made a mistake in the books. It was because of her inexperience. It was her first real job. She was only eighteen and had never done any bookkeeping before. Douglas accused her of stealing. She panicked. I panicked. I went to see him on her behalf…' She bit her lip as if the memory upset her. 'I begged him not to press charges…'

Marc felt as if a giant hand had gripped his intestines. 'So he offered you a way to get your sister off the hook.'

She nodded, her features contorted in a grimace. 'It was the only way to pay back the money that had gone missing. I had no one else to turn to. Our father and stepmother wouldn't have helped either of us. I was so worried about Serena. She's not like me. She's fragile. I felt I had to protect her. I still feel I have to protect her.' She gave him a pleading look. 'Please, you mustn't tell anyone about this. Not even Richard knows.'

'Did you ever think to approach me for help?' Marc asked, not quite able to take the edge of bitterness out of his tone.

She gave a sigh that involved her whole body. 'I thought of it, but you hadn't contacted me since I had left the apartment. Then just as I was about to call you I read about you in one of the papers. You were dating again. I saw the photo of you with her. She was very beautiful.' She gave him a look that made his insides clench even more. 'Dark and exotic…nothing at all like me.'

Marc swore viciously in both Italian and French. 'You little fool,' he said roughly. 'I was only using her to make you jealous. Little did I know that less than a week or two later you would be married to someone else.'

She looked away, but he was almost certain he had seen the sheen of tears in her eyes. He took a steadying breath, trying to think, trying to clear the cloud of confusion and regret and recrimination inside his head.

'Our relationship,' he said after a moment. 'This thing we have going on between us…'

'What exactly is going on between us, Marc?' she asked. 'Blackmail, that's what.

This is all wrong and you know it. It's been wrong from the start.'

'I can make it right,' he said, seriously wondering if he could. 'We could start afresh. We can forget about the past. We can pretend we've just met for the first time.'

She shook her head at him. 'Another game, Marc?' she said. 'Well, let me tell you something. I am tired of rich men's games.'

He frowned at her. 'This is not a game to me, Ava. I want you in my life. I thought I had made that clear.'

'Yes, you've made it very clear. The trouble is, I don't like the terms,' she said, and giving him an embittered look, marched past him to leave, her slim body encased like a small Egyptian mummy in the bed sheet. It heeded her progress, which was just as well, as his mind was working so slowly she might have got away before he could put his hand out to block her.

'Ava, wait,' he said, taking her hands in his. She had such tiny hands, he felt them fluttering inside the cage of his, like small, frightened sparrows.

He cleared his throat, trying to find the words to say what needed to be said. 'I didn't know all the facts before. What you've told me…well, it makes a world of difference. We can work it out, *cara*. Somehow we'll work it out.'

Her slim brows rose. 'Isn't it a bit late to right the wrongs of the past?' She clenched her teeth and added, 'One phone call from you and none of this would have happened. Do you realise that? One phone call. It's been *five* years, Marc. Five years of my life have gone and I can't have them back.'

'I know how long it has been,' he said heavily. God, he had felt every bitter second of them eating away at him. Why had he allowed his pride to do such damage? Why hadn't he gone to her? To think he might have prevented the last five years of hell, not just his, but hers, with just one phone call or a text or a simple e-mail was like mental torture. Why had he let his father's experience dominate his life to such a degree? And how could he ever turn things around? She hated him and had every right to for that and that alone. How could he expect her to ignore the past and move on? She had told him she had been friends with Cole, but what if that hadn't always been the case? What if she had suffered at his hands—maybe not physically, but what about emotionally? Marc knew all about the way people could destroy each other with emotional abuse. He had seen it happen before his very eyes; the stripping away of self-esteem and loss of power had devastated his father and flowed on to him, leaving him with wounds that still tugged at him deep inside like scar tissue.

'You've always been so vocal about your hatred of Douglas, but you exploited me just as he did,' she said. 'He used me to get what he wanted and you could have stopped it, but you didn't.'

Marc looked at her, for the first time in his life no words came to him. She was absolutely right: he was exactly like Cole. He had exploited her and ruined both of their lives in the process. The knowledge of it was like poison in his gut. He felt his insides churning with it. It was like spilt acid, eating its way through him, burning him with a pain like no other.

She pulled out of his hold with a strength he had no idea she possessed. 'I am going to have a shower,' she said, her eyes still flashing their daggers at him. 'I feel dirty all of a sudden.'

Marc let her go. Her words were like a slap—they stung long after she had left the room, echoing in the silence, like ghosts from the past coming back to haunt him....

* * *

It had taken hours for Ava to get to sleep that night. Once she had cooled down after her heated conversation with Marc, she had lain awake, vainly dreaming of him coming to her room and gathering her in his arms and pleading for her forgiveness for not begging her to come back to him after she had left that first time. If he had cared anything for her, wouldn't he have fought just a little bit for her? But then, she had always known Marc was a proud man. He wasn't the type to beg or plead. He hated being vulnerable and he hated being wrong. How he would deal with what she had told him was yet to be seen. But she had a feeling he would not be offering her anything permanent in the way of the future. He said he wanted her in his life, but those were the exact words he had used five years ago. They were temporary words, not forever words.

Marc was nowhere in sight during the following day and Celeste just shrugged distractedly when Ava asked if she knew where he was. 'I am not feeling well, *madame*,' Celeste said, putting a hand to her forehead. 'I think I am coming down with that virus you had.'

'Go home and rest,' Ava said. 'Take the rest

of the week off. I am perfectly capable of cooking a meal or two.'

'Are you sure?' Celeste looked worried. 'Signor Castellano… Last time I saw him he seems…how you say…not quite himself?'

Ava forced a smile, but it felt more like a grimace. 'He'll get over it. You know what men are like—they like to brood over things for a bit.'

'He's a good man, *madame*,' Celeste said. 'You are much more suited to him than to Monsieur Cole. Signor Castellano will be a good husband and a wonderful father to your children, *oui*?'

Ava felt her heart tighten like a vice. 'Don't get your hopes up, Celeste,' she said. 'Marriage has always been a bit of a no-go subject with Marc.'

Celeste pursed her lips thoughtfully. 'Some men need more time to get there than others,' she said. 'Don't give up on him. He has come this far to have you back in his life.'

Ava sighed once the housekeeper had left. She resigned herself to another day of waiting and hoping for something to cling to, some sign that Marc was not going to end their relationship before it had even had a chance to start. It was the same as five years ago; the same anguished feelings of insecurity constantly plagued her. Would this be the day—or tomorrow, or the next day—she would see him for the last time? How could she live like that? She wanted so much more. She wanted forever.

When she came downstairs later that evening, Marc was standing near the drinks-preparation area, a drink of something amber-coloured in a tumbler. His expression was as difficult as ever to read, although Ava thought he looked tired about the eyes, as if he had not slept well the night before. There were lines of strain etched at the sides of his mouth as well, making her want to reach up and stroke them away with her fingers and to press her mouth to the flat line of his to ease away its tension.

'Can I get you a drink, Ava?' he asked. 'You look like you could do with one.'

She self-consciously tucked a wisp of hair back behind her ear. 'Do I?' she asked. 'Why do you say that?'

He lifted one shoulder. 'You look a little pale. Have you had anything to eat today? I'm not sure what arrangements have been made about dinner. I can't seem to find Celeste.'

'I gave her today and the next couple of days off,' Ava said. 'I hope you don't mind, but she wasn't feeling well. I think she's caught the same stomach virus I had before. It takes ages to shake off. I still don't feel one hundred per cent and it's been weeks.'

'How are you feeling now?' he asked, his eyes moving over her in concern.

She placed her hand over the queasy puddle of her stomach. 'I'm fine…I think…'

He set about pouring a drink for her, his movements measured and slow, as if he was rehearsing something in his head. 'I am sorry about last night,' he said as he finally faced her. 'I haven't handled this very well, have I?'

Ava was hard pressed to know if he was deliberately distancing himself preparatory to ending their short-lived affair. She took the glass he handed her, but she found her stomach turned at the taste of it as soon as she put it to her lips.

'What's wrong?' he asked. 'Would you like some water or some ice with it? From memory I thought you used to like it straight.'

She handed it back to him. 'Sorry, Marc, I'm not really in the mood for a drink.'

He put her glass to one side, meeting her gaze once more. 'I spent today working on some business,' he said. 'I thought you might be interested in hearing about some decisions I've made.'

Ava sat on the edge of the nearest sofa, even though with him still standing it made her feel at a disadvantage, but her legs felt unsteady and her stomach was still curdling. 'Oh? What sort of decisions?'

He looked down at the contents of his glass for a moment before returning his gaze to hers. 'I have set my legal team to work on drawing up a trust fund for Cole's children, Adam and Lucy. I have also organised some funds for his ex-wife. She won't have to work again unless she wants to.'

Ava stared at him, her heart beating so loudly she could hear a faint roaring like the ocean in her ears. 'That's…that's very generous of you, Marc,' she said. 'I am sure they will appreciate the gesture.'

He gave an indifferent lift of one shoulder as if he couldn't care either way what they thought. 'It seemed the right thing to do, and God knows I have not always done the right thing in the past.'

Ava pressed her hands between her knees,

wondering if he was leading up to something.

There was a beat or two of silence before he asked, 'What does your sister know about us?'

She met his penetrating gaze even though it made her cheeks grow warm. 'I told her we were back together. I didn't want her to feel guilty about what had happened. She has enough on her plate to deal with.'

He studied her features for a moment. 'So you didn't tell her about our deal?'

Ava gave him an ironic look. '*Our* deal? Your deal, Marc, not mine. You know very well if it wasn't for the money I wouldn't be here for a moment longer than necessary.'

He twirled the last of his drink, his expression wry. 'Ah, yes,' he drawled. 'The money. It always comes back to the money.'

'What are you getting at?' she asked, feeling her hackles start to rise at his tone.

'It's pretty simple, isn't it?' he said. 'You needed money, I wanted a mistress. A fairly straightforward transaction, or so one would have thought.'

Ava decided to be straight down the line with him. 'If you are unhappy with the services so far then please say so. I would hate to be causing you any dissatisfaction.

After all,' she injected her tone with reproach, 'you paid a fortune for me.'

He put his glass to one side and came up to her, lifting her face with one fingertip beneath her chin. 'I am very happy with the services, as you call them,' he said, looking deeply into her eyes. 'Very happy indeed.'

Ava wished she had the strength or where-withal to pull away, but with his light touch on her face, and his dark-as-night eyes locked on hers she felt ambushed by her feelings for him. This was the time to be putting some distance between them. She knew she should put her hands against his chest and push him away, but somehow she couldn't do it. She rehearsed each of the steps in her head, she even got as far as raising her hands, but instead of pushing him away, as soon as her hands felt the hard contours of his chest, she felt as if she had come home. She felt the strong, steady beat of his heart against her palm, and the blood in her own veins began to race. Her tongue flicked out over her lips in nervous anticipation, her heart hammering inside her chest, her legs feeling as if they were not bones and ligaments and muscles and tendons, but two pipe-cleaners without their wires. She felt the rest of her body sway towards his, her mouth opening on a breathless little sigh as his warm breath caressed the surface of her lips, her heart coming to a screeching stand-still when his mouth came inexorably closer, closer and closer until finally sealing hers.

CHAPTER EIGHT

Ava wound her arms around Marc's neck, giving herself to his kiss with a sigh of deep, shuddering pleasure. His tongue stroked for entry and then roved the moist cave of her mouth, finding all the sensitive nerve-endings that made her cling to him all the more.

His hands skimmed her breasts, his light touch sending off shooting sparks of awareness as her nipples sprang to attention. His kiss deepened, one of his hands going to the back of her head, cupping the nape of her neck as his lips and tongue drove her crazy with longing.

His other hand worked on her clothes, lifting her top, unclasping her bra so he could cup her breast in the warmth of his hand. She pressed against him, her nipple rock-hard, the feel of him exploring her making her flesh pepper all over with goose pimples.

Ava stroked her hands down his back, pulling his shirt from his trousers so she could feel the warm silk of his skin beneath her fingers. He groaned into her mouth as she moved to his buttocks, her hands cupping him tightly, holding him against the heart of her need.

She felt the hard ridge of his erection, and quickly released the waistband of his trousers, desperate to hold him, to caress and stroke the satin and steely length of him.

He sucked in a sharp breath as she finally freed him. She ran her fingertip over him, teasing him with circular motions until he pulled her hand away with a growl that sounded primeval and intensely male.

He pressed her to the rug on the floor, dispensing with clothes and shoes with breathtaking haste, pausing only to retrieve a condom from his wallet in the back pocket of his discarded trousers.

Ava shivered as he came over her, his weight pinning her, his arousal probing for entry, but gently this time, holding back until he was sure she was ready to receive him. She relaxed her pelvis, opening to him, drawing him in with a hitching sigh as he filled her, his thickness smooth and sure as it finally and fully claimed her.

She felt every thrust against her sensitive inner muscles, each one rippling over him as he drove a little harder and faster. His mouth covered hers with a searing kiss, his tongue mimicking the thrusts of his lower body, sending her senses into a spinning vortex of feeling. She felt the tension build and build inside her, like climbing a high mountain in anticipation for the spectacular view at the top. Step by step she was getting there; each movement of his body in hers made the journey all the more exhilarating. She heard his deep groans, each one as it rumbled through his chest against hers making her pleasure all the more intense. She hovered at the pinnacle, her body desperately seeking that final plunge into paradise.

Marc sensed her need and used his fingers to coax her over the edge. He loved the feel of her in full arousal, the soft silk of her, the swollen heart of her pulsing against his fingertips as she finally let go. He felt each of her spasms, heard each of her startled gasping cries as her orgasm swept her away. She shuddered and shook and thrashed beneath him until he could hold on no longer. With a grunt he surged into her, losing all thought, all he could do was feel. The sensations flowed through him, the hot wave of release that left him lying in the blissful shallows of lassitude.

'Am I too heavy for you?' he asked into the silence of the aftermath.

'No,' she said softly, her fingertips tracing a feathery pathway up and down his spine that made every hair on his head stand on end in pleasure.

Ava sat up and hugged her knees to her chest, affording herself a small measure of dignity, considering she was in the middle of the sitting room with not a stitch on. 'You really are dead set against having a child, aren't you?' The words were out of her mouth almost before she had realised she had been thinking them, let alone about to say them. It was too late to take them back.

His eyes cut to hers, dark and inscrutable. 'I realise this must be a sensitive issue with you given what your sister is going through, but yes, I am not interested in having a child.'

Ava felt annoyed at his dismissal. It was so easy for men; they could put fatherhood on hold indefinitely. She on the other hand had felt her biological clock ticking like Big Ben ever since she had turned twenty-five. Nearly three years had passed since then and she was rapidly approaching thirty. She had read the statistics: female fertility dropped alarmingly after the age of thirty-five. The thought of ending up alone and childless was unbearable to her. For as long as she could remember Serena and she had shared a deep longing for true love and a little family to call their own.

Ava gathered her clothes and struggled back into them, suddenly desperate to get some time alone, to think about what she should do. She was back right where she had started with Marc. He was unwilling to compromise in any way. She would always be the one to make the sacrifices. She had made so many already, how could she continue to give up her hopes and dreams indefinitely?

'I would like us to dine together this evening,' Marc said. 'Take your time getting ready. The restaurant at the casino will not mind how late we are.'

'I'm not hungry.'

'Then you can watch me eat because I am.'

'There is plenty of food in the kitchen,' she said. 'Help yourself.'

'I want you to come with me, Ava. I've told you before, it is important that we are seen together.'

Her top lip curled at him in contempt. 'So dining out is nothing more than a publicity stunt?'

'If you want to see it that way, but I would much rather view it as a chance to relax and get to know one another again over good food and good wine.'

Her eyes fell away from his, her bottom lip subjected to a savaging by her teeth that he was certain would draw blood.

He stepped towards her and brushed his thumb over her mouth. 'You must be hungry after all,' he said with a wry smile.

She gave him a fierce little scowl as she moved out of his reach. 'I don't feel like going out. I want to go to bed.'

He gave her a glinting smile as he reached for her again. 'Then that is where I will take you.'

Ava quickly stepped backwards but the sudden movement made her head spin crazily. Her stomach roiled with nausea, her whole body feeling clammy. A swirl of ghastly coloured patterns formed in front of her and she felt as if she was going to drop in a faint. She fought to hold on to consciousness, but her legs started to wobble.

'Are you all right?' Marc asked, steadying her with a hand on each of her forearms.

Ava swallowed back a mouthful of sickness. 'I…I think I've had too much sun…or something…'

Marc swept her up in his arms and carried her towards the staircase, ignoring her paltry pleas to put her down. 'No, I will not put you down,' he said. 'You can barely stand up as it is. I am going to call a doctor. You have obviously had a relapse of that stomach virus. You must have caught another bout of it from Celeste.'

Ava was suddenly too weak to fight him. Besides, there was something rather comforting about him taking charge. She felt the protective strength of his arms around her and wished she could stay like that forever.

Once he got to the bedroom he laid her down on his bed, and with gentle fingers smoothed her sticky hair off her face. 'Who is your regular physician?' he asked.

'I'm sure I'll be fine in a minute,' Ava said weakly. 'I just need to rest.'

He gave her an intractable look and picked up the handset from the bedside table, and in rapid-fire French had a medical service agreeing to a house call within the half hour. 'Now,' he said, replacing the phone in its cradle, 'I am going to get you a drink of water and something to eat.'

Ava felt her stomach heave. 'No food… please…no food…'

He looked down at her with a heavy frown. 'If you were feeling so unwell, why didn't you say so when I first came home?' he asked.

Ava plucked at the hem of the sheet he had covered her with. 'I was feeling all right then…'

He let out a deep breath as he sat on the edge of the bed. He picked up her hand and brought it up to his mouth, holding it against his lips while his eyes held hers. Ava wondered what he was thinking. He was studying her so intently; it made her feel on edge, as if any moment he was going to drop a bombshell on her.

The doorbell sounded and Marc released her hand. 'Stay put,' he commanded. 'I will bring the doctor up.'

Ava lay back on the pillows with a sigh. Her hand felt cold without the warm cradle of his, her heart empty without the promise of his love. Tears smarted at the backs of her eyes, but she fought them back, angry at herself for being so needy. Why couldn't she just let things take their natural course? He would no doubt tire of her within a month or two. She could move on with her life, maybe one day meet someone else. She choked back a sob, suddenly overcome with emotion. She didn't want anyone else. She had only ever wanted Marc. She blew her nose hurriedly as she heard footsteps approaching, and stuffed the tissue under the pillow as the door opened.

The doctor was in his mid-fifties and, after brief introductions, quickly and efficiently took a history. Ava felt self-conscious with Marc standing there listening to every word, but she answered the doctor's questions as best she could.

'What about your periods?' the doctor asked. 'Have you missed any lately?'

'Um…I'm on the sort of Pill that stops menstruation altogether…'

The doctor looked at her over the rim of his glasses, which were perched on the middle of his nose. 'Have you been taking it regularly?'

'Y-yes.'

The doctor tapped his pen against his lips in

a thoughtful muse. 'Have you been ill recently? A stomach upset, vomiting or the like?'

Ava swallowed tightly. 'Yes…'

'Have you had unprotected sex recently?'

She felt her face heating and lowered her gaze back to the hem of the sheet, but before she could answer Marc had answered for her. 'Yes,' he said, 'just the once, about two weeks ago.'

The doctor pulled out a tourniquet and blood sample kit. 'I'll do a blood test to make sure,' he said. 'The results will be back in a couple of days.'

Marc spoke again. 'I would like to know the results as soon as possible.'

The doctor gave him an as-you-wish movement of his lips. 'I will mark it as a priority,' he said.

Marc saw the doctor out and while he was out of the room Ava got off the bed and went to the bathroom. She washed her face, pausing for a moment to examine her reflection. She was hollow-eyed and pale, but surely it was just the result of long weeks of nursing a terminally ill patient on top of a persistent virus. She dared not think of an alternative explanation, but even so one of her hands crept down to the flat plane of her belly and lingered there…

'Ava?'

She turned as the door opened. 'Do you mind?' she asked. 'Am I not allowed any privacy?'

'We need to talk.'

She pushed past him irritably. 'Too bad. I don't feel like talking.'

Marc took her by the arm and turned her to face him. 'Ava, this is a situation we have to face like two adults.'

Ava tugged herself out of his light grasp, pointedly rubbing at her arm as if he had hurt her. 'This is your fault,' she said, struggling against tears.

'I know it is,' he said in a low deep, tone.

She looked up at him in surprise.

He sent one of his hands through his hair, the only hint he was feeling out of his depth. 'I want you to know that if you are pregnant I will support you. You don't need to worry about the baby's future. I will make sure you and he or she are always well provided for.'

Ava ran her tongue over her dry lips. 'It's probably a false alarm…'

His dark eyes locked on hers. 'But what if it's not?'

She snagged her bottom lip with her teeth, her forehead crinkling in a frown of worry. 'If it's not, I don't know how on earth I am going to tell Serena.'

Marc studied her expression for a moment. 'You don't think she would be happy for you?' he asked.

She looked at him with her misty grey-blue gaze. 'It's seems so unfair,' she said in a whisper-soft voice. 'She's been trying to get pregnant for four years. How can I tell her I got pregnant by accident?'

Marc came over and placed his hands on her shoulders. He hated it when she flinched at his touch, but he knew he had only himself to blame. He had held her to ransom from day one. If she hadn't hated him before she surely did now. For a fleeting moment he had wondered if she had engineered this situation to her advantage, but one look at her tortured features made him realise he had once again misjudged her. She didn't want a permanent tie to him. She had told him outright. She was happy to take his money, but that was all she wanted from him.

Marc forced his thoughts back to the problem at hand. 'We don't know for sure if you are pregnant,' he said. 'But I am sure your sister will be happy for you in spite of her problems.'

She slipped out of his hold and crossed her arms over her chest, making him feel as if she was shutting him out. 'I can't believe this has happened…' She started to pace the floor. 'It's like a nightmare. I keep thinking someone is going to tap me on the shoulder and wake me up.'

'Ava, please stop pacing for a moment,' Marc said. 'You should be resting.'

She looked at him with antagonism in her gaze. 'You sound like a concerned father-to-be, but we both know this is not what you want. You've never wanted it. The last thing you want is a permanent tie to me, and you can't get much more permanent than a living, breathing child.'

He came over to her and, although she tried to resist, he soon had her hands in his. 'Listen to me, Ava. I know I have handled things badly. I know you are angry and upset and feeling uncertain. But I need you to forgive me for my part in how things turned out. I know it's asking a lot of you and I know I don't deserve it.'

Ava hovered in that dark place between uncertainty and hope. She looked into his unfathomable eyes and wondered if he was backing down because of the possibility of her being pregnant. He was an only child. He had no living heir. How convenient would it be for him to pretend to have feelings for a woman he had mistreated in the past just because she could be carrying his child? It seemed a little too coincidental that on the very day a pregnancy was suspected he came with apology in hand. 'I need some time to process this,' she said, once again pulling out of his hold.

His jaw worked for a moment as if he was fighting to keep in control. 'If you are pregnant I insist we marry immediately.'

Ava felt her mouth fall open. 'Pardon?'

He gave her a trenchant look. 'I do not want any child of mine to be called a bastard.'

'For your information it won't make much of a difference,' she shot back.

'I mean it, Ava,' he said. 'I will not be shut out of my child's life.'

'You said you never wanted a child.'

'That was before.'

She arched her brows. 'Oh? So what has changed?'

'Things are different now. Everything is different.'

Ava was not ready to capitulate so readily. 'I don't want to rush into anything. You weren't prepared to marry me before. Why should I accept a proposal that has been forced out of you by circumstances instead of out of genuine desire?'

'I will not be shunted to one side,' he said through gritted teeth. 'Don't mess with me, Ava. I will take the child off you if I need to. You wouldn't stand a chance in court, not with the way the Press has savaged your reputation over the years.'

Ava realised with a sickening jolt he was right. Taking on an opponent such as Marc was asking for a very public, very humiliating defeat. She had thought she still loved him, but right at that moment her hatred of him was immeasurable. It pulsed through her like a raging tide, sweeping away every poignant memory, every precious moment they had spent together.

It was war and he was determined to win, but she was not going down without a valiant fight.

She lifted her chin and aimed her knock-down punch where she knew it would hurt the most. 'You seem pretty convinced the baby I might be expecting is yours. Isn't that a little presumptuous of you under the circumstances?'

A lightning-fast zig-zag of anger lit his gaze as her words hit their target. It was a long moment before he spoke, the stretching silence so weighted Ava felt it pressing down on her chest like a concrete hand.

'I suppose I deserve that,' he said heavily. 'But I will not insult you by requesting a paternity test.'

Ava's mouth fell open again. 'You…you won't?'

He shook his head. 'Knowing what I know about you now, I have no reason to believe the child is anyone's but mine.'

Ava narrowed her eyes. 'Is that because you've had me tailed for weeks on end or because you genuinely believe I don't sleep around?'

His gaze remained steady on hers. 'Ava, this is not helping anything by bringing up the mistakes of the past. If we are to make a success of our relationship we will both have to let go of bitterness and blame.'

'I don't want to be railroaded into anything without first giving it careful thought,' she said, pulling on a wrap and tying it securely about her waist.

'I will not settle for anything but marriage,' he said with an intransigent set to his features.

She gave him a look of defiance. 'Then you have got a huge task ahead of you, Marc Castellano, because I am not marrying you.'

'Damn it, Ava, if you don't marry me I will ruin your family and your friends, every single one of them,' he said through white-tipped lips. 'Don't think I won't do it to get what I want.'

Ava felt the cold, hard determination of his words freeze her to the spot. Her heart beat sickeningly, each beat like a blow to her chest. He was ruthless enough to do anything. Hadn't he already proved it? He had forced her into his life as his mistress and now that the stakes had changed he wanted to rewrite the rules. He wanted control, absolute, total control. 'Black-mail is not the way to get a girl to agree to be your wife,' she said in a voice that was not quite steady. 'Anyway, aren't you jumping ahead a little? I might not even be pregnant.'

'It doesn't matter. We will be married regardless.'

'Why the sudden change of heart?' she asked, unable to keep the echo of suspicion out of her tone.

His dark eyes gave her no clue as to what he was thinking, although she could see a flickering nerve at the side of his mouth. 'There are some things I need to do in order to correct the mistakes of the past,' he said. 'Marrying you is one of them.'

Ava let out a breath of disdain. 'I can see why you failed the entrance exam to charm school. That has got to be the most appalling proposal I have ever heard.'

'What do you want me to say, God damn it?' he asked. 'I could wrap it up in flowery words and phrases but you wouldn't believe it for a second.'

'You're damn right I wouldn't,' she shot back.

He let out a harsh-sounding breath and, turning away from her, shoved a hand through his hair again. When he finally spoke his voice had lowered to a deep burr. 'I will make arrangements for us to marry in London later this month. It will save your sister from having to travel.'

'You can make all the arrangements you like, but it's not going to make me say yes,' Ava said with a furious scowl.

His eyes met hers across the room. 'You might want to have a rethink about that, *ma belle*,' he said. He came back to where she was standing and lifted her chin with two of his fingers, his voice lowering to a silky drawl. 'Don't fight battles you have no hope of winning.'

'You can't make me love you,' Ava bit out petulantly.

His gaze devoured hers as the silence lengthened, moment by moment, heartbeat by heartbeat. 'That is not a requirement of this arrangement,' he said, dropping his hand from her face.

'You're prepared to marry a woman who *hates* you?' she asked.

He gave her an inscrutable flicker of his lips that could have almost passed for a smile. 'If nothing else it will be a delightful challenge to make you change your mind.'

She pulled her shoulders back and sent him a flinty glare. 'Then you've got one hell of a task ahead of you.'

'I know.' He bent down and planted a hot, hard kiss to her tight mouth. 'I am looking forward to it.'

Ava watched in silence as he left the room, the soft click of the door as it closed, an ominous reminder of what he had promised and how determined he was to achieve it.

CHAPTER NINE

WHEN Ava came downstairs the next morning Marc was on his way up carrying a tray with tea and toast, and a folded newspaper under his arm.

'Why are you out of bed?' he asked. 'It's only just seven.'

Ava eyed him suspiciously. 'I'm not an invalid and I always get up early.'

'I know, but you deserve breakfast in bed, surely?' he said.

She folded her arms. 'Why do I get the feeling this is all part of a scheme to get me to agree to your plans?'

'Why do I get the feeling you are fighting me just to prove a point?' he returned.

Ava blew out a breath and continued on her way downstairs. 'I'm not hungry.'

'You have to eat, Ava,' he insisted as he followed her down. 'You've got to think of the baby.'

She swung around at the foot of the stairs and glared at him. 'There probably isn't a baby. Then what will you do? Retract your proposal?'

He put the tray down on the hall table and handed her the newspaper. 'It's a bit late for that,' he said. 'I've already released a Press statement.'

Ava stared down at the section he had folded the paper to. Her heart knocked against her rib cage as the words leapt off the page at her: *'Grieving widow to wed Italian construction tycoon.'*

She thrust the paper to his mid-section, taking some measure of satisfaction in the little grunt he gave as her hand connected with his abdomen. 'Then you'll have to retract it because I am not marrying you.'

'Damn it, Ava, you have to marry me.'

'Why?' she asked with a hand on one hip. 'Because otherwise you're going to ruin my family and every other person I know and love? I don't think so, Marc. You might be a bastard at times, but you're not that big a bastard. In any case, I am tired of being a pawn in rich men's games. If you want me to marry you then you will have to do it the old-fashioned way.'

Marc ground his teeth together in frustration. 'What would it take to get you to change your mind?'

She rolled her eyes at him. 'You shouldn't have to ask!'

He thrust his hand through his hair, leaving it messier than it had been before. 'Ava.' He cleared his throat and began again. 'I know I should have probably told you this before, but I had a miserable childhood. I know it's more or less fashionable these days to claim you've been stuffed up by your parents' behaviour, but in this case it's true.'

Ava felt her stiff stance ease as she watched the play of emotions on his face. She could see how hard it was for him, the bitterness he felt was written all over his face. She could see the pain in his dark eyes, the frown lines on his forehead bringing his brows almost together.

'My parents divorced when I was seven,' he said in a voice she barely recognised as his. 'But for the next three years I watched as my father was repeatedly and publicly humiliated by my mother's behaviour. She seemed to take some sort of perverse pleasure in dangling each of her toy-boy lovers in his face on every access pick-up. I was sickened by it. I was nothing but a pawn in her game. I don't think she had the capacity to love a child, or at least not the way a child deserves to be loved. She loved money and living in the fast lane much more. I was an inconvenience, a hindrance that she couldn't wait to get rid of.'

'Oh, Marc…'

He held up a hand. 'No, let me finish,' he said. He took a ragged breath and continued. 'From the age of ten, when I saw my father drown himself in alcohol after my mother's death, I swore I would not let any woman do to me what had been done to him. In the end he lost everything he had worked so hard for. The business that had been in our family for generations went bust, he owed money everywhere. I had to work three jobs while I was still at school and then four while I was at college to pay off the debt after he died.'

Ava bit her lip until she tasted blood. Her heart ached for the little boy he had been, for the pain and rejection he must have felt, for all he had suffered. How he must have hated her for marrying Douglas. It all made such perfect sense now. She had ruined him just as his mother had done to his father. No wonder he had come looking for revenge. 'Oh, Marc…' she said again.

'I know I should have told you this before,' he said. 'I should have told you before I set you up in that apartment in London. I know you wanted more and God knows you certainly deserved more. If I could rewrite the past I would do it, but I can't.'

'It's all right,' she said softly. 'I understand.'

He gave her a weary look. 'I'm not a good bet, Ava, but I can promise to take care of you and the baby. You have my word on that. You will not want for anything as long as I am alive.'

Ava didn't like to tell him that what she wanted most could not be bought with money. It was enough that he had shared this small part of his heart with her. He had revealed his past in a way he had never done before.

She stepped back to him and placed her arms around his waist. 'Thank you for telling me,' she said, looking up into his eyes. 'I am so sorry you had such a hard time as a child. No child deserves that sort of pain. No ex should hate their partner more than they love their child.'

His hands slipped around her back and pressed her closer. 'Are you still dead set against breakfast in bed?' he asked with a hint of a smile.

'I hope the toast hasn't gone soggy.'

He scooped her up in his arms. 'Let's go see, shall we?'

Ava woke from a blissful sleep an hour or so later. Marc was lying on his side, watching her. She reached out and touched him to make sure she wasn't dreaming. His flesh was warm and hard and her heart squeezed as she thought of how he had pleasured her earlier.

He touched her face lightly. 'You have a linen crease, right there,' he said.

Ava felt it with her fingers and grimaced. 'I must look a fright. I need a shower.'

His eyes darkened as he held her gaze. 'Why not join me?'

Ava felt the delicious thrill of anticipation trickle through her as he led her into the *en suite*. He set the water temperature and stepped in, taking her with him. His arms went around her, holding her against his growing erection. She relished the surge of his blood against her, her body quivering as he bent his head to hers.

The cascading water added a sensual

element to the kiss. He cupped her face in his hands, his mouth exploring hers in exquisite detail, his tongue playing with hers, making it dance around his with excitement as her passion rose.

His hands moved down from her face to cup her breasts, his thumbs teasing each of her nipples before he bent his mouth to each one in turn. Ava leaned back against the marble wall, a river of delight running through her body as his lips and tongue worked on her sensitive flesh. Her feminine core pulsed with longing, her legs barely able to keep her upright as Marc's mouth slowly but surely travelled via her shoulders and neck before taking her mouth under his again. This time the kiss had more urgency in it. She felt the hard probe of his body nudging her and she opened her thighs, sighing with bliss as he teased her at her moist entrance. She became brazen with him, reaching down and touching him, circling him with her hand, rubbing and stroking while she was swallowing each of his groans.

He pulled away from her mouth, looking down at her with glittering eyes so black with desire her insides twitched with heady excitement. 'Turn around,' he commanded.

Ava felt another thrilling wave of anticipation course through her as she turned her back to him. She shuddered when his hands gripped her by the waist, the feel of him behind her, so hard, so engorged, so powerful and so ready, made her shiver all over.

The difference in their heights was no barrier. Ava lifted herself on tiptoe as he bent his long strong legs, thrusting into her with such slick force she gasped out loud. 'Tell me if I'm going too fast for you,' he said in a gruff, passion-filled voice.

'You feel amazing,' she breathed.

'God, so do you,' he said, nuzzling at her neck. 'I love feeling you like this. I can feel every part of you holding on to me.'

Ava rocked back against him, anchoring herself against the marble wall of the shower, giving herself up to the powerful sensation of having him move within her. He upped his pace, the deep, thrusting motion making her flesh tingle all over. Her breathing became ragged as the tension grew inside her, her heart beating faster and faster. It was so incredibly intimate feeling him like this, her bottom pressed up against his lower abdomen, her feminine folds swollen and super-sensitive as he drove into her, time and

time again. Every nerve-ending was screaming for release, every part of her seemed to be
marshalling for that final plunge into
paradise.

Marc seemed to be fighting his own battle
to maintain control. Ava knew he was close
to bursting, she could hear it in his breathing
and she could feel it in the urgency of his
thrusts as the water poured down over their
rocking bodies.

Ava suddenly felt the trigger go on her
control. It caught her by surprise, sending
her into a cataclysmic roller-coaster ride of
sensation. Her nerves felt as if they had
exploded with feeling, each and every one of
them vibrating like the strings of a violin
played by a master. It went on and on,
making her feel as if she had shattered into
a thousand pieces and would never be the
same again.

She was still breathless in the aftermath
when she felt Marc prepare to come. He
thrust harder and harder, his deep groans
sounding so sexy she knew she would live
with this erotic fantasy in her head for the rest
of her life. She felt him burst with release, the
pumping action of his body sending her flesh
into a shiver of rapturous delight.

He held her against him as his breathing steadied, the water washing away his seed from her body. Ava wondered if he realised he hadn't used a condom, but thought against mentioning it. She didn't want to spoil the intimacy of the moment. She had never felt so close to him and yet he had still not mentioned anything about his feelings for her. She didn't want to repeat the mistakes of the past and hound him for assurances, even though she desperately wanted them.

He turned her around and kissed her mouth, softly and lingeringly, his hands moving up and down her body in a caress that was as fluid as the water coursing down upon them.

After a while he reached past her and turned off the shower. He didn't speak; he just picked up a towel and began to dry her as one would do to a small child. Ava gave herself up to his ministrations, enjoying the tenderness after the mind-blowing passion they had shared.

Their eyes met.

Ava tried to keep her emotions in check. She didn't want to appear needy or clingy. That would be the ultimate turn-off for him. She affected a casual demeanour, keeping her voice light and carefree. 'What are your plans for the day? I thought I might go to the gym and then do some reading for the course I'm planning to do.'

He reached for another towel and roughly dried himself before tying it around his hips. 'I have some bookwork to pore over,' he said, watching her closely. 'And I have a wedding to plan. Why don't you give your sister a call and tell her the news before she reads about it in the papers?'

Ava kept her face impassive. 'I thought I'd wait until we hear from the doctor. No point rushing into things.'

He held her gaze for a throbbing pause. 'You are determined to make me beg, aren't you?'

'You don't strike me as the type to beg for anything, Marc,' she said, reaching for a bathrobe.

He blew out a breath as he followed her into the bedroom. 'What do you want from me? I've offered to marry you. That's what you always wanted, wasn't it?'

Ava rolled her eyes before she faced him. 'I am not going to be browbeaten into a loveless marriage. I've already had one of those, remember?'

The phone rang at the bedside and Marc snatched it up impatiently. 'Marc Castellano,' he clipped out.

'It's your sister,' he said, handing it over.

Ava took the phone, watching as Marc grabbed at some clothes before he left. 'Serena…' she said. 'I…I was going to call you.'

'It's OK,' Serena said. 'I know things must be a little crazy for you right now. Marc sounded a bit curt just then. Is everything all right?'

Ava felt tears sting at her eyes, but valiantly fought them back. 'I suppose you read the news. He wants us to get married.'

'That's a good thing, isn't it?' Serena asked. 'I mean, you still love him, don't you?'

Ava bit her lip and took a deep breath before she answered. 'That's the problem. I love him but he doesn't love me.'

'How do you know he doesn't?' Serena asked. 'Has he said something to the contrary?'

'No, it's just our relationship has always been about…about other things,' Ava said, trying not to think about what had just happened in the shower. 'He's only offering to marry me now because…' She stopped, wondering how she could frame it to some-how lessen the blow.

'Is there a possibility you could be pregnant?' Serena got in first.

Ava let out a sigh that shook its way through her chest. 'I'm not sure… I've had a blood test.… I'm waiting for the doctor to call with the results.'

There was a little silence.

Ava could imagine how her sister was feeling. She could imagine the ambiguity of feeling joy and envy for someone you loved, wanting something so much that it hurt to hear of others succeeding where you had failed.

'Ava, I am so excited for you,' Serena said.

'You are?'

'But of course, silly,' Serena assured her. 'What, did you think that I would be upset or jealous or something?'

'Well, the thought had crossed my mind…'

'Ava, you've done so much for me, it's about time something went right for you for a change,' Serena said. She waited a beat before adding, 'Richard and I have decided to have a break from IVF. We are so grateful for all you've done to help us financially, but

Richard feels uncomfortable taking any more money off you.'

'But darling, you can't stop trying,' Ava said. 'You'll get pregnant again. I'm sure of it.'

'I am hopeful of it, but right now I think Richard is right,' Serena said. 'We've spent our whole marriage focusing on me becoming pregnant. It's put us under enormous pressure, both emotionally and, of course, financially. We want to pay you back. I'm going to get a job and in a couple of years we're going to try again. I'm not like other women, who have their age against them.'

'Are you sure about this?' Ava asked. 'The money's not an issue. Marc has given me—'

'I don't want you to sacrifice yourself for me any longer,' Serena said adamantly. 'I feel worried that you might not be telling me the truth about your relationship with Marc. It's just the sort of thing you would do, like you did with Douglas. You made me believe you were happy about the arrangement and I guess because I wanted to believe it I went along with it. But no more, Ava. I want you to be genuinely happy. No one deserves it more than you.'

Ava blinked back tears. 'I don't know what to say…'

'How does Marc feel about the possibility of a baby?'

Ava gave another sigh. 'It's been a difficult time for both of us. It wasn't what either of us expected.'

'Is there anything I can do? What about coming over to stay for a while? If you are pregnant we could go shopping for baby things. It would be fun. It's just what I need to stop thinking about my own stuff.'

Ava chewed at her lip. Maybe some time with her sister would be a good idea right now. She couldn't think with Marc around her, tempting her into marrying him for all the wrong reasons. The more time she spent with him the harder it was to say no. 'It does sound nice…'

'I'm sure Marc will agree,' Serena said. 'Anyway, you have to buy a wedding dress. I can help you. It will be much more fun this time around.'

Ava didn't have the heart to tell her sister she couldn't bear the thought of another white wedding. Instead she promised to call as soon as she had heard from the doctor and rang off.

The phone had hardly been back on the cradle when it rang again. Ava stared at the number in the call-ID screen, recognising it as a local one. She picked it up and answered, her stomach folding over when she heard the doctor's voice.

'The results of your test were negative,' he said after greeting her by name. 'But you do, however, have a slightly lower than normal blood count, which would account for the symptoms you are experiencing. I suggest you take an iron supplement for a few weeks, that way if you do plan a pregnancy you will be in much better health to carry it to term.'

Ava hung up the phone a short time later, her thoughts whirling. Disappointment sliced through her; she hadn't realised how much she had hoped for a positive result until now. She put her hand on her belly, an ache of longing filling her until she felt as if she wanted to curl up and howl.

The door opened and she looked up to see Marc standing there with a questioning look on his face. 'Was that the doctor?' he asked. 'I was outside and couldn't get to the phone in time.'

Ava fought back her emotions with an effort. 'Yes, it was.'

'And?'

She searched his face, wondering if he would be able to disguise his relief when she told him.

'Ava?' he prompted. 'What did he say?'

She took a little breath. 'He said I'm anaemic. I have to take a supplement.'

The air seemed to be sucked out of the room as the silence lengthened.

'So you're not pregnant?' he asked, his expression still giving nothing away.

She shook her head. 'No.'

'Could it be a mistake?' he asked. 'What if they got someone else's results? It happens sometimes. People's names and birthdates are similar, so—'

'Marc, I am not pregnant, OK? You're in the clear. There's not going to be a baby.'

He slowly let out the breath he had been holding. 'How do you feel about it?' he asked.

She frowned at him. 'How do you expect me to feel?'

'I don't know,' he said. 'I thought your greatest desire was to have a baby.'

'Under the right circumstances, yes—but not like this.' She turned away and began to leave the room.

'Where are you going?' he asked.

She turned and faced him with a challenging look. 'I'm going to pack.'

His brows snapped together. 'Pack for where?'

She lifted her chin. 'I'm going to stay with my sister. I want some time, Marc. You can't stop me from going.'

'Aren't you forgetting something?' A hard look came into his eyes.

Ava's hand gripped the doorknob. 'I don't need your money, Marc. Serena's not having any more IVF for a while.'

'What about the debts Cole left behind?'

She gave him stare for stare. 'I don't care about the debts. If you want to take me to court then fine, go right ahead. I'll find some way of dealing with it. I just want some time to think about my life, about where I go from here.'

Marc kept his hands clenched by his sides as he fought the desire to reach for her. He knew he had to tread carefully. So much was riding on how he responded. He had to fight every urge to force her to stay with him. Threats came to mind, horrible threats he would never, ever act on, but he left them unspoken. He didn't want her to hate him any more than she already did. Although for a time there he had wondered... He gave himself a get-a-grip shake. She only responded to him because sex was the language he had always spoken with her. He had to take it out of the equation, to see if there was anything else they could build a relationship on. It would be hard, it would be painful, it would tear him in two to let her go, but he would have to do it, to make sure if she came back it was what she wanted, not just something she had no choice in.

It was unfamiliar territory for him to feel so utterly, so helplessly vulnerable. 'I'll give you a month,' he said, stripping his voice of any hint of what he was feeling. 'But that is all. One month, no contact other than by phone or e-mail—then you can't accuse me of trying to coerce you into it.'

She seemed to consider it for a moment. 'A month...' Her tongue sneaked out to moisten her lips. 'O...K...and...and after that?'

'After that if you don't want to continue our relationship you will be free,' he said. 'I will not force you to marry me. You will never have to see or hear from me again.'

CHAPTER TEN

'AVA, THAT'S THE THIRD morning in a row you've been sick,' Serena said. 'Are those iron pills you've been taking disagreeing with you?'

Ava wiped her face with the hand towel her sister had handed her. 'God, I feel so ghastly.' She clutched at the basin as another wave of nausea hit her.

'You know, if it hadn't been for the fact you haven't been anywhere near Marc for the last month, I would swear you were pregnant,' Serena said, handing her a face cloth. 'Maybe you should do another test. Perhaps the blood test was wrong.'

'Blood tests are supposed to be far more reliable than any other test,' Ava said as she mopped her face and waited for the sickness to ease off.

How could she be ill on the very day she was

supposed to meet Marc? She had wanted to look and feel her best. She had missed him so much; she had counted the hours until she would see him face to face again. He had phoned her a couple of times a week, but she had found it hard to talk to him. He seemed aloof, distant, as if he was already moving on without her. She had read every paper and gossip magazine, but there had been no sign of him out and about with anyone else. She took some measure of comfort in that, but it wasn't much. Maybe he was waiting until the month was up to get back to his playboy lifestyle.

'I know this is a very personal question, but did you happen to have unprotected sex with Marc since the blood test was taken?' Serena asked.

Ava met her sister's eyes in the mirror above the basin. She swallowed, and then, as if drawn there by a magnet, her eyes went to the shower stall. It was nothing like the luxurious one at the villa in Monte Carlo. For one thing there were tiles instead of Italian marble, and the water had a tendency to gush hot and cold unexpectedly, but each time she had stepped into the cubicle she had thought of Marc and that passionate interlude.

'Ava?'

Ava gave herself a mental shake and focused back on Serena's questioning gaze. 'Do you have any left-over pregnancy tests?' she asked.

Serena opened a cupboard with a flourish. 'Take your pick. I have eight different brands.'

Ava took the first one her hand touched. 'This is probably going to be negative. I'm on the Pill, for God's sake.'

'Yes, but only a low-dose one,' Serena reminded her, 'and they are not one hundred per cent reliable.'

Ava bit her lip. 'Give me a minute, OK?'

Serena smiled and, blowing her a kiss, closed the bathroom door.

Ava opened the bathroom door a few minutes later. 'You're not going to believe this…' she said, clutching the dipstick in her hand.

Serena squealed and began to jump up and down in excitement. 'Oh, my God!'

Ava bit her lip, torn between wanting to laugh and wanting to cry. 'I'm supposed to be meeting Marc tonight for dinner. Tonight's the big night. I'm supposed to give him my answer.'

'Honey, you didn't need to do a pregnancy test to confirm you're going to go back to him,' Serena said. 'I've known what your decision was from the moment you stepped in the door a month ago. Richard saw it too.'

Ava grimaced sheepishly. 'Was I that obvious?'

Serena smiled. 'Dreadfully, tragically, just like in the movies. It's a wonder Marc couldn't see it for himself.'

Ava sighed as she rested her hand on her belly. 'I miss him so much. I can't believe I went five years without seeing him. How on earth did I survive that?'

Serena wrapped her arms around Ava and hugged her tightly. 'I wish the last five years hadn't happened. I will always feel guilty about that. You gave up so much for me. I can never repay you.'

Ava returned her sister's embrace. In the four weeks she had been in London she had noticed a difference in Serena. Sometimes Ava felt like the younger sister. Serena had become protective of her, instead of the other way around. 'You don't owe me anything,' she said. 'Anyway, it's time to put it behind and move forwards. The past belonged to others, the future belongs to me.'

* * *

The hotel they had arranged to meet at was where they had first met. Ava wondered if Marc had chosen it deliberately or whether it was just a coincidence, or even a matter of convenience. She knew he stayed at that particular hotel a great deal, as it was close to his office tower. He had been photographed numerous times over the years with other women in the same bar.

She took a deep breath and walked towards the bar, her heart beating way too hard and too fast as she searched for him amongst the other people gathered there. The pianist was playing a romantic melody, one that made Ava feel as if she was travelling back in time. But this time it was different. There was no tall figure leaning indolently against the bar, no dark, unreadable eyes meeting hers across the clot of other drinkers.

Ava felt her stomach sink in panic. He hadn't come. He had forgotten… No, he had decided he didn't want her any more. He had found someone else, a glamorous new lover who didn't want kids and commitment.

She glanced at her watch. She was late, not early. Was this his final revenge? To leave her dangling as she had done to him all that time ago?

Her teeth sank into her bottom lip, her eyes sweeping the bar again and again. Her panic turned to despair. She felt as if she was going to cry. Tears gathered and threatened to spill, and her chest ached with the effort of holding herself together.

'Ava.'

She spun around at the sound of that deep, unmistakable, mellifluous voice. 'Marc…' Her voice came out on a croak. 'I thought….' She blinked a couple of times. 'I thought…' She swallowed and just stood staring up at him.

Marc took her hands in his. 'Sorry I was late. I got stuck with a phone call.' He bent and pressed a light kiss to each of her cheeks. 'You look very beautiful.'

Her lips fluttered with a nervous-looking smile. 'So…how are you?'

He tried to smile back but it felt false. His chest was pounding and his skin had broken out in a sweat as if he were on his first date. 'I'm good, and you?'

'Er—fine…good…really good.' Her gaze fell away from his.

Marc felt a tight hand around his heart. He

was losing her. She could barely look at him. 'So...you're not anaemic any more?' he asked.

'Er—no,' she said, blushing like a rose.

A silence swirled around them.

'Would you like to have a drink in the bar?' Marc asked, wishing the bar weren't so crowded, wishing he had thought to meet her somewhere else, somewhere more private. But he had hoped to recreate that moment when they had first met. It was a rather pathetic attempt to rewrite the past. There was no way either of them could do that, least of all him.

She shook her head and slowly raised her eyes to his. 'Could we go somewhere a little more private?'

'Sure.' He pulled out his room key, hoping she didn't notice how his hand was shaking. 'I have a permanent suite here, so we can go upstairs.'

Marc could see how uncomfortable she was with him. He tried to compose himself, but it was so hard with her within touching distance. He could smell her perfume, that alluring fragrance of summer flowers that had haunted him for the past month, let alone the past five years.

He had found the last month unbearable. It had brought home to him how much he needed her. He had restricted his contact to twice-weekly phone calls to keep from begging her to come back to him then and there. The dreadful thought of never seeing her again, or—worse—seeing her with someone else had eaten away at him until he had nearly gone mad. He had barely slept; he had barely been able to function in order to get through each day. And then there was the disappointment about the pregnancy. He was still struggling to overcome that blow. How had his feelings changed so swiftly? Now all he could think about was a little baby, a dark-haired boy who looked like him or an adorable blonde little girl, the image of her mother. He looked at Ava again, his heart contracting at the sight of her standing there, chewing on her lip as if she couldn't wait for this to be over.

The doors of the lift opened and Marc led her to his penthouse. She moved past him in the doorway, her slight frame brushing up against him, setting every nerve on edge. 'Can I get you a drink?' he asked.

'Marc, there's something I have to tell you…' she began.

'No,' he said, closing the door behind him. 'Let me go first. Please, I need to say this. I've been rehearsing it for the past month.'

She looked a little uncertain. 'O…K…'

He came over and took her hands in his again, his thumbs stroking the backs of her fingers gently. 'Firstly, I have to tell you something that I think will be quite upsetting to you.'

He saw the flicker of panic in her grey-blue eyes and the tip of her tongue as it darted out to sweep over her lips. 'Go on…'

'Your sister didn't make any mistakes in the bookwork,' he said. 'That was a set-up by Cole and very cleverly hidden by Hugh Watterson. Cole wanted the Dubai account and he conjured up a scheme to make sure he got it. He knew about our relationship from various articles in the Press. Serena was on his staff, so it was too good an opportunity to miss. When you broke off our relationship he made his move. By blackmailing you into marriage he won over the vendor's confidence. He had the money to splash around on a young, beautiful wife who had chosen him over me. I didn't stand a chance in the vendor's eyes. I wasn't even in the same ball park.'

She closed her eyes as she took in the information. He could feel the tension in her hands as she held on to him. She opened her eyes again and looked at him. 'So…so I never needed to marry him?' she asked in a choked whisper.

Marc shook his head. 'I'm sorry. I know that's nowhere near good enough to make up for what you went through, but I am so deeply sorry for not coming after you when you left. I will never forgive myself for that. I let you down in the most unforgivable way.'

She pulled out of his hold, hugging her arms around her middle, her expression contorted with bewilderment as she began to pace the floor. 'I can't believe it… How can people be so cruel? He never once told me. He could have told me before he died. He *should* have told me. Serena had a right to know. For God's sake, *I* had a right to know.'

'Maybe he was frightened if he told you, you would leave him to die alone,' Marc said. 'God knows, it was what he deserved.'

'He set me up.' She looked at him again. 'He set you up too and made you hate me.' Her face crumpled then, tears sprouting in her eyes. 'That was the worst part. Knowing you hated me so much.'

Marc felt emotion clog his throat. 'I don't hate you, Ava.'

She blinked again as if his words hadn't quite registered. 'You…you don't?'

He shook his head. 'Why do you think I came after you and forced you into a relationship with me?'

She pressed her lips together, thinking about it for a moment. 'I thought you wanted revenge…'

He came over to where she was standing, unpeeling her arms from around her waist so he could hold her in the circle of his arms. 'I thought so too,' he said with a rueful look. 'I convinced myself I was intent on making you pay for what I thought you had done. But looking back now, I realise what I was really doing was giving myself another opportunity to start over with you. I wanted to make you fall in love with me the way I had fallen in love with you five years ago.'

Ava had to shake her head to make sure she wasn't misinterpreting what she had just heard. 'You were in love with me? The whole time you were in love with me?'

'I know this sounds crazy, but I didn't realise how much I loved you until I thought I was going to lose you the second time,' he said. And, wincing, added, 'Go on, say it. Tell me it's too late, that you're well and truly over me. I can take it. I've been preparing myself for it for the last four weeks. It's no more than I deserve.'

Ava felt a smile slowly spread across her face. 'You think that's what I'm going to say?'

He made an effort to look as if it didn't matter, but this time she could see through it. She saw the way his throat constricted as he tried to disguise a swallow, and the way a little nerve pulsed at the side of his mouth. His eyes too had become dark and glistened with the suspicion of moisture. 'I can take it, Ava,' he said. 'You don't need to wrap it up to soften the blow. I didn't exactly treat you with any consideration for your feelings.'

'I love you, Marc,' she said, trying not to cry. 'I have never stopped loving you… Well, maybe for a week or two here and there.'

He tightened his hold, his eyes dark and intent upon hers. 'You're not just saying that, are you? I'm not going to do anything about the debts Cole left behind. I would never have held you to account for those. I just had to find a way to keep you with me.'

'Oh, Marc,' she said, hugging him tightly. 'Why have we wasted so much precious time?'

He buried his head in her hair. 'Don't let's waste another minute. Let's get married as soon as we can and then we can start on trying for a baby. I was so disappointed when that test came back negative. Besides the fact it left me with no bargaining tool to keep you with me, I got to thinking about what it would be like to have a child. Everywhere I looked I saw young couples with a baby or a little child. It seemed so right all of a sudden.' He held her from him to look at her. 'What do you say? Do you feel ready to have a baby with me?'

Ava felt her heart swell inside her chest. 'You want a baby?'

He gripped her even tighter. 'Think about it, Ava, a baby who looks like both of us. A little person who will grow up with so much love they will have the best start in life possible. We won't make the mistakes our parents made. I will make sure of it.'

'Oh, Marc,' she said almost unable to speak for the wave of love that encompassed her. 'I have the best news for you. You won't believe it—I can barely believe it myself.'

'Try me.'

She nestled against him. 'Remember the shower?'

He gave her a smouldering look. 'How could I forget? I've relived that in my head every day for the past month.'

'Well, you did more than share a shower with me,' she said. 'You left a memento.'

A light came on in his eyes. 'Are you serious? You're pregnant? Really?'

She smiled. 'Are you pleased with yourself?'

He grinned back at her. 'Yeah, pretty much. So I guess this means you're not going to say no to marrying me.'

Ava threw her arms around his neck. 'I wouldn't dream of it,' she said and closed her eyes in bliss as his mouth met hers.

LARGER-PRINT BOOKS!

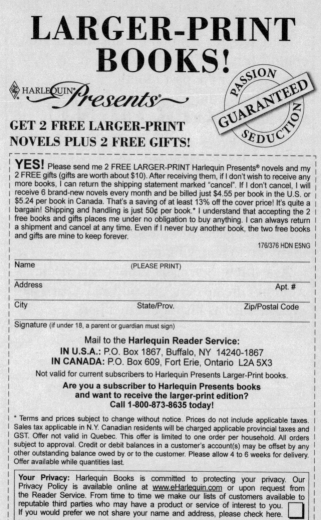

HARLEQUIN *Presents~*

PASSION
GUARANTEED
SEDUCTION

GET 2 FREE LARGER-PRINT NOVELS PLUS 2 FREE GIFTS!

YES! Please send me 2 FREE LARGER-PRINT Harlequin Presents® novels and my 2 FREE gifts (gifts are worth about $10). After receiving them, if I don't wish to receive any more books, I can return the shipping statement marked "cancel". If I don't cancel, I will receive 6 brand-new novels every month and be billed just $4.55 per book in the U.S. or $5.24 per book in Canada. That's a saving of at least 13% off the cover price! It's quite a bargain! Shipping and handling is just 50¢ per book.* I understand that accepting the 2 free books and gifts places me under no obligation to buy anything. I can always return a shipment and cancel at any time. Even if I never buy another book, the two free books and gifts are mine to keep forever.

176/376 HDN E5NG

Name	(PLEASE PRINT)	
Address		Apt. #
City	State/Prov.	Zip/Postal Code

Signature (if under 18, a parent or guardian must sign)

Mail to the **Harlequin Reader Service:**
IN U.S.A.: P.O. Box 1867, Buffalo, NY 14240-1867
IN CANADA: P.O. Box 609, Fort Erie, Ontario L2A 5X3

Not valid for current subscribers to Harlequin Presents Larger-Print books.

Are you a subscriber to Harlequin Presents books
and want to receive the larger-print edition?
Call 1-800-873-8635 today!

* Terms and prices subject to change without notice. Prices do not include applicable taxes. Sales tax applicable in N.Y. Canadian residents will be charged applicable provincial taxes and GST. Offer not valid in Quebec. This offer is limited to one order per household. All orders subject to approval. Credit or debit balances in a customer's account(s) may be offset by any other outstanding balance owed by or to the customer. Please allow 4 to 6 weeks for delivery. Offer available while quantities last.

Your Privacy: Harlequin Books is committed to protecting your privacy. Our Privacy Policy is available online at www.eHarlequin.com or upon request from the Reader Service. From time to time we make our lists of customers available to reputable third parties who may have a product or service of interest to you. If you would prefer we not share your name and address, please check here. ☐

Help us get it right—We strive for accurate, respectful and relevant communications. To clarify or modify your communication preferences, visit us at www.ReaderService.com/consumerchoice.

HPLP10R

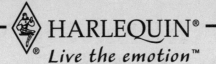

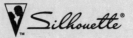

Harlequin® Historical
Historical Romantic Adventure!

Imagine a time of chivalrous knights and unconventional ladies, roguish rakes and impetuous heiresses, rugged cowboys and spirited frontierswomen— these rich and vivid tales will capture your imagination!

Harlequin Historical . . . they're too good to miss!